Mercury Off Course

Steve Rzasa

Books

Urban Fantasy
Mercury On Guard
Mercury For Hire
Mercury At Risk
Mercury Is Hot
Mercury Out Cold
Mercury Off Course

Space Opera
The Word Reclaimed: The Face of the Deep 1.0
The Word Unleashed: The Face of the Deep 2.0
Broken Sight: The Face of the Deep 2.5
The Word Endangered: The Face of the Deep 3.0
Severed Signals
Cryptic Commands
Failed Frequencies
Mixed Messages
Empire's Rift: A Takamo Universe Novel
Strife's Cost: A Takamo Universe Novel

Science-Fiction
Man Behind the Wheel
Multiverse
For Us Humans
The Echo Watch

Superhero
Airfoil: Origins

Fantasy
The Bloodheart
The Lightningfall
Just Dumb Enough (contributor & editor)

Steampunk
Crosswind: The First Sark Brothers Tale
Sandstorm: The Second Sark Brothers Tale

CHAPTER ONE

March

I bashed through the shoji paper screen before the Syndax mercenaries could sacrifice the family they'd kidnapped.

Don't ask me why the soldiers had a middle-aged dad and mom, plus two teen-aged boys, spread out on the polished granite floors like the world's biggest wingless butterflies. I wasn't so much interested in the whys as the hows—as in, how was I going to stop the murder of four people. And also, the what.

The what being the massive machete a mercenary in full tactical armor slashed down at the dad's chest.

Bamboo and shredded translucent paper exploded into the dingy confines of the abandoned restaurant. A blast of gold and white energies from the pulsar stave melted the machete in mid-swing. Molten steel sprayed the soldier's arm, rewarding me a with a big angry scream.

The spray also stained a garish wall painting of a sumo wrestler, vaporizing his hideous grin. Talk about tacky. No wonder Black Lotus had been closed for a year. That and, you know, the twenty cases of food poisoning had turned it from San Camillo's latest sushi restaurant into a boarded-up business on the Promenade facing the bay.

"It's him!" Two of the mercenaries swung around, automatic rifles aimed.

Yeah, it's me.

Mercury Hale, resident monster slayer and occasional foiler-of-crime, trying to enjoy his first few months of marital bliss. I should have been home with Loredana, making sure the TV was streaming *Dr. Who* re-runs while we cooked up a batch of shrimp po-boys.

Instead, one abnormal tachyon spike later, I was swinging my weapon at the helmeted head of a guy who probably should have stayed in jail or picked up a gig as a nightclub bouncer. Working for an evil syndicate with ties to the previously-mentioned monsters was not gonna look great on his resume.

That single strike put the first of my opponents face-first into a booth. Something cracked. Plastic? Bone? I didn't care. What mattered was that he and his other seven compatriots were focused on me, instead of the four sobbing victims.

Make that five. There was a black lab straining against his bindings as he whined and snapped at the nearest soldier.

"Are you kidding me?" I blurted. "You're gonna kill the dog, too? Guys, there's villain and then there's *villain.*"

Guns crackled to life.

Big surprise. But maybe those clowns hadn't seen me in action before. They sure weren't expecting me to blast out of their line of fire as bullets shredded chairs and splintered tables behind where I'd been standing. My supersuit was a motley display of black and gray patterns crammed together, with blazing lines of yellow light illuminating the edges. The suit's intricate technology siphoned the pulsar stave's power, enhancing what I could draw from the weapon and storing it for lots of fun purposes. Like moving super-fast, which to be fair, I didn't need the suit to do.

Or camouflage.

I blended into the restaurant's background, little more than a hazy, transparent figure against the ugly furnishing and even uglier artwork. Seriously. If you ever meet a white guy from North Dakota who thinks it'd be a great idea to open an ethnic restaurant, save him and twenty people the stomachache. Tell him *no*.

"Forget him!" The voice that shouted the command between the fusillades had an edge of pain to it. Probably because the guy's hand was suffering blistering burns from his melted machete. "We have the sacrifices. Initiate the rip."

Hang on. The rip? That was Procyon Foundation lingo—as in, the term for a breach between this world and the nasty, monster-filled dimension known as the Interstice. You could get to a lot of other realms by taking a transit through the Interstice, but I wouldn't recommend it for a vacation. Unless you wanted to die.

"Hey, Mercury!" The voiced stabbed through my earbud. If it'd been a person sneaking up on me, I would have stabbed it. Him. Her. Whatever.

"Bad time, Liz." I whispered. Not that I needed to, with these goons insistent on shooting up every square inch of upholstery in hopes of perforating me.

"Oh! Wow, I've got those thirteen heat signatures the drone's recording and a whole new set just bloomed but they're not as diffuse as a person's body temperature so I figured it has to be guns and then I heard over the earbud—"

"Liz! Stay on target!"

A silhouette stepped in front of the shoji screen four feet in front of me. I blasted through with the stave, then hurtled into the sizzling remnants, stepping on the knocked-over body and leaping horizontally at the next guy.

I caught a glimpse of eyes as black as night fringed in glowing purple.

Whoops.

The mercenary swung his weapon too fast for me to avoid. The blow struck my shoulder and sent me careening over the stainless steel chef's station.

Forgot. These guys liked to juice with a Syndax Multinational concoction—tachyon-infused astral fiend goo. Monster blood, basically. It would amp their strength, temporarily. Not sure what the side effects were.

Didn't matter in the middle of a fight like this.

"Garvey and Wilhelmina are on their way!" Liz yelped into the earbud. "But I don't know how soon. SCPD has barricades going up at either of the Promenade."

"Great. More potential targets for these jokers." I said this upside down. Took a second to get righted, even as a mercenary rounded each end of the counter like human versions of the barricades Liz had just mentioned.

I let them both get unobstructed fields of fire before I separated the pulsar stave into two pieces of equal length emblazoned with intricate carvings and slapped both against the damp tile.

A sparking shockwave sent both men tumbling like leaves blown down the sidewalk. Good deal. I was evening the odds.

And better yet, when I leapt back over the counter, I saw no one had tried to fillet the kidnapped family. The dog was still snapping at anyone who got to close. As much as I wanted to free him and let him join the fracas, I knew they'd shoot him dead before he could do much damage.

Which left things up to me, as usual. At least until my backup could arrive.

The soldiers stopped shooting. Burnt Hand, their leader, reached onto his back and drew a second machete. Because of course he had a spare. "Don't think you can stop the inevitable. We will appease the hungry to gain access to our fallen."

A gust of wind blew through the restaurant—or rather, blew out from it. Scraps of mildewed menus flitted across the floor and over tables. The wind whipped into a mini cyclone, gathering speed near the door to the kitchen.

Purple lightning skittered around the frame.

"That sounds terrible." I tensed, the staves' power coursing through my body like a second circulatory system, running side by side with my blood. Every heartbeat urged me to launch into their midst. I was on the wrong side of the family. The Syndax boys said they wanted a sacrifice and, apparently, that involved stabbing, but I wasn't gonna chance them using plain old-fashioned guns if I made the wrong move. "Since everybody I've sent into the Interstice hasn't come back, why don't you rethink that plan?"

"It is your doing. We mean to undo the damage. You've deprived us of our leaders."

"Yep. And good riddance. But hey, if you want to keep talking, keep talking."

A shadowy form spun through a booth, colliding with the leftmost mercenary as it entered the lit area of the restaurant. No ninjas on Procyon's payroll. Wilhelmina was just as agile when she wielded her dagger, a long, slender blade forged in my home dimension of Meda. She landed atop the man's chest and slashed the blade through his gun, leaving the halves tinged with glowing red. The dagger sparked with gold-white, like the pulsar staves, courtesy of the tachyon enhancement module Liz had rigged to its hilt.

"Here I though you was the one who did all the jabbering." Wilhemina's voice was warm and soothing, like a grandma offering cookies. You know, like the Oracle, from *The Matrix*. Not ninja material. A perfect fit for a short, stocky black woman in her seventies, though.

If you think my appearance startled the cult-in-training, Wilhelmina's really threw them for a loop. The mercenaries glanced back and forth between the two of us, looking like they were debating whether to take on the costumed Millennial or the Baby Boomer wearing red-striped exercise pants and a zipped-up fleece jacket, both midnight black.

Turned out, the astral fiend ended their internal debate.

The rip, well, ripped the barrier between Earth and the Interstice, disgorging a slobbering monster that bumped its head against the ceiling. I used the term "head" loosely. The astral fiend was more of a ten-foot-long lump of knobby hide, a dark violet with spikes protruding from eight tentacles. Three misshapen eyes glowed blood red over a gaping mouth packed full of fangs. He could have swallowed any one of us whole.

First thing the fiend did was shriek so loudly everyone, bad guys included, covered their ears, because *ow*.

Except for Burnt Hand. He raised his dagger, eyes

crazed with—fervent devotion? Abject terror? Too much tachyon steroids? All three, I'd guessed. "For the Whisperer and his servants!"

I was already moving.

I'd slid across the floor, alongside the family. The pulsar staves cut their leg bindings as I passed them. Wilhelmina copied my move and freed their hands.

But the dagger plunged into Burnt Hand's chest, not his intended victims'.

Never did find out if an astral fiend preferred sacrifices to live prey, because the fiend wrapped Burnt Hand in a pair of tentacles. His cry cut through me worse than the fiend's, even though it lacked the volume. I spun around and threw a stave, a clean shot that severed one of the tentacles. Wasn't enough to prevent my enemy's death, though. The fiend drained his life from his body in seconds, reducing what had been a musclebound, armor-clad mercenary into a shriveled mummy, empty eye sockets and all.

The twin boys screamed in unison and everyone snapped back into action.

"Come on, y'all!" Wilhelmina seized the mom's collar and dad's sleeve, dragging them out of the line of fire—because those idiot Syndax guys started shooting again. Bonus: They were emptying their magazines at the astral fiend instead of the family or me or Wilhelmina.

"Guess it's not so fun summoning the devil when he actually shows up," I muttered.

I took the opportunity to yank the twins clear, in

the opposite direction, but I figured since they were teens I could do so with more gusto. They wound up across a divider between tables, landing on a heap of discarded seat cushions.

Then there was Fido. Excuse me—I squinted at his collar. "Agamemnon?"

He bared his fangs.

"Easy, Agamemnon." I flicked the stave across his tether and jumped back, as an astral fiend tentacle whipped above my head. "Go protect your owners."

The lab barked, then pounced at the nearest tentacle, pinning it to the ground. He pulled on that sucker like he'd found a new chew toy fresh out of the box.

Screams echoed from the fiend.

Great. Now the dog was gonna get himself killed!

"Hey, Liz!" I shouted over the gunfire. I slashed through a tentacle and spun through the air, whirling toward where my other pulsar stave half had landed. One of the mercenaries picked it up and pointed it at me. No dice. It was just a dead stick of metal to someone who didn't possess the genetic code of a Medan descendant.

As in, a person born in another dimension.

"Garvey's in position! He's at the railing opposite the Black Lotus entrance!" Liz yelped. "Get the fiend outside and he can reverse the rip!"

Those were a lot of exclamations for one statement, but since shouting was the way to go, I wasn't gonna complain. I landed in front of the mercenary. He seemed befuddled by the inactive stave.

"Here, let me." I grabbed the end he was pointing at me and sent a surge out the backside. It flashed against his chest and put him deep into a shoji screen, his boots protruding from between splintered bamboo posts.

Another hideous cry—the fiend had found a second meal. Thankfully, it wasn't the family. I glimpsed Wilhelmina herding them out a broken window at the front of the restaurant. The astral fiend cast aside the limp, uniformed body of a Syndax mercenary. Don't get me wrong. His death was as sickening as if it'd been the innocent victims I'd come to protect. But those guys should know better than to mess with monsters. Fiends weren't big on taking requests from anybody outside of the Interstice.

That left me, two Syndax mercenaries who'd ran out of ammo, and a furious Labrador intent on avenging his owners.

"Okay, Agamemnon. Heel!" I caught the dog as the astral fiend whipped its tentacle toward me. Oof! Beefy boy. He about knocked me off my feet. But I siphoned pent-up energy from the suit and hurled the pup like a discus toward the front. His howls faded as he arced through the same window the family exited. A meaty collision of flesh against flesh, followed by cries of surprise, pain, and joy told me I'd hit the target.

So, I threw a dog. Get over it.

I sliced through the tentacle, but two of the previously severed were already growing back, and the fiend looked like he'd put on weight. As in, grown by a couple feet in all directions and sprouted handfuls of fangs.

That was enough for the Syndax boys. They bolted through the front door.

"Not a fan of multi-tasking," I muttered. "Wilhelmina, do me a favor and trip up the two who dined and dashed."

"Be glad to oblige. You need help? Want me to come on back in?"

The astral fiend charged.

I brought the stave back together and held it out as a shield, pouring its energies from the suit. The burst of light reassured me but didn't stop the freight train that was one outraged fiend. He collided with me and my attempted barrier.

The impact exploded the front wall of the restaurant, spilling us and the shattered remnants out onto the Promenade.

Any other night, I'd have enjoyed being there. Maybe when vendor booths full of local artisans crammed the boardwalk between storefronts and metal railings, or when musicians had fans packed into the bars and cafes. But the Promenade was empty. As was every other venue in town.

That was the deal when your city was locked down because of the COVID-19 coronavirus. Look, I hadn't checked off "pandemic" on the New Year's

Eve bingo card, but you roll with it.

There were police barricades way down either end. Red and blue lights flickered. But at least SCPD wasn't shining floodlamps to illuminate the scene. Which meant Lt. Gabriel Ramos was kindly keeping my masked face and general likeness out of the public eye and off the interwebs.

A tentacle snaked around my waist.

"Yeah, no thanks." I severed it, pinwheeled the stave toward the fiend's yawning maw—

It slapped aside my attack and plowed into the boardwalk's surface. Timber snapped as it burrowed through wood planks as easily as a kid digging a trench in the sand. Where the heck was it going?

Right toward Wilhelmina, and the family extricating themselves from Agamemnon's happy, bounding licks.

"Garvey!" I flung myself atop the fiend and stabbed deep into its hide. The monster roared but kept on its rampage. My boots slipped, but I hung on to the stave. "Do it!"

A purple glare flashed from the shadow by the railing. It hit the fiend, halting its advance a car's length out of reach of the family. Wilhelmina parried the tentacles. I dumped the stave's power into the fiend but couldn't get deep enough to its core to kill it.

Finally, the familiar windy crackle of a rip opening filled my ears. I could hear the portal stretching itself across the restaurant, streaming out onto the Promenade and reaching for the fiend.

Garvey stepped nearer, muscles in his arms bulging through the gray compression shirt as he steadied the portal emitter—big old device, like a radar gun triple the normal size. Handy for shoving astral fiends back into the Interstice when they proved finicky.

Which this one surely did.

Suddenly the rip expanded, and my ride dissolved, its form disintegrating as it screamed itself to oblivion. Which meant I fell right through the giant hole torn in the boardwalk. I bounced off planks, slammed into a piling—

And the beam dropped on me.

It pinned me to the slope of the shoreline, a crushing, nauseating pain that would not let up. I thought I'd pass out. Kind of wished I could. But the agony was unforgiving.

Water rushed over my head.

In an instant, I was drowning. No time to catch my breath. The pressure unrelenting. I could only see a glassy blur. Debris pelted me from all sides.

Airfoil. He was overhead, somewhere, a white flash here and there lost an instant behind the bits and pieces that were dropping from the sky.

I wasn't gonna die down there. Not after all this.

But I was, if I didn't get free. I couldn't push it off or worm from underneath. I hacked at the beam with the ax's blades, but it was too thick. Switched to the energy-blade end of the pulsar stave. No luck.

Blackness pressed in on the sides of my sight.

One way out.

I twisted the stave-ax one last time. Its energies fizzled as my consciousness started to bleed away. Soon it'd be useless, because I'd be knocked out.

So, I cut.

The intense heat was as bad as the pain of the crushed limb. I ignored it, clawed my way through the water, wondering if I'd bleed to death or suffocate first—

A hand grabbed mine. I broke the surface of the dark churning water. I couldn't catch my breath. "Don't—don't let go."

"Mr. Hale? Sir, hold still! Stop thrashing."

Sir? Who had me? I couldn't see. I punched against him, struggling to get free, even as he swam me toward the banks underneath the boardwalk.

That's where I was, right? Not on the pier outside the destroyed Procyon Foundation headquarters. Not drowning at the end of our fight against the Hedron of Orbits. Not cutting off my leg to stay alive.

"Easy. Sir." Garvey dragged me onto the bank. "Mr. Hale. Can you hear me?"

"I … Yeah." I wiped water from my face. Hands wouldn't stop shaking. Heart couldn't stop pounding. "The fiend?"

"Gone, sir." Garvey brushed mud off his nose. "But so are the Syndax guys—the ones not dead, that is."

"Then we've got to—" I tried standing up, but my legs gave out. I collapsed, shuddering, my mind a jumble. "I can't. I can't."

Garvey touched his earpiece. "Wilhelmina? Get the family clear and meet me at the truck. I'm calling for a medic."

The rest of their exchange was a muddle of nonsense. I couldn't get focused.

I was full-blown terrified.

CHAPTER TWO

The blank concrete wall was pitted and crumbling. Rusted pipes peeked out of jagged cracks. Down in the abandoned Titan-II missile silo in the hills north of San Camillo, nobody at Procyon Foundation's hidden and temporary base had time for redecorating. Either that, or it wasn't in the budget.

I didn't mind staring at the rundown façade. Took my mind off reliving the horror of nearly dying.

"Blood pressure's come down." Doctor Arne Becker ripped the Velcro open and tossed the cuff onto the wheeled tray parked next to the exam bed. "Heart's calmed, too. You were in tachycardia when they brought you back."

"I guessed." My chest ached, but at least I could breathe again. That, and I wasn't shaking in terror anymore.

What was wrong with me?

"He was fine before he went in the water." Garvey

stood at the foot of the bed, arms folded, big as a semi except made of out human muscle. He hadn't budged since he'd helped a pair of medics wheel me in on a stretcher, if you can believe it. "When I pulled him up, he was punching at me. I thought I might have to subdue him."

I snorted. "We get it. I lost my nerve for a second. No big deal. It was a fluke."

"Fluke? That's funny. It's pronounced 'post-traumatic stress disorder.' Or so I learned in medical school." Doc Arne's slick handlebar moustache twitched as he scowled at us, making the young physician—as in, my age—appear twice as old and triply cranky. "Hence the P, H, and D. Does anyone else in here have those letters after their name?"

"No need to get all snippy." Wilhelmina leaned against her cane at the bed next to mine. The knitting bag festooned with a very colorful cat clashed with her nighttime monster-fighting attire. She patted my hand. "Ain't every day a body goes through the same fright as the one that almost ended his life."

"Glad you're all having fun diagnosing me." I hopped off the bed. My head didn't spin and I didn't go into a dry-mouthed panic. I pulled on a gray T-shirt featuring Procyon's double black parallelogram and silver star logo over the left breast. "Not going crazy. I had a flashback."

"You had a panic attack, one brought on by plunging into identical circumstances that nearly killed you five months ago," Arne said.

"So what? It happens."

"Not to you. Not in the middle of a fight. Sir." Garvey watched me like a parent expecting the next temper tantrum.

Okay. If they wanted one, I was ready to dish, after all the physical prodding and verbal poking. "Listen up, guys—"

"There's no need to protract the debate or the diagnosis." Loredana walked into the infirmary in time, as usual, to prevent me from embarrassing myself. Which usually happened when I opened my mouth. She was dressed in gray slacks and a pale-green blouse, professional, but not ready for a day at the office.

"Hey. How was dinner?" I kissed her cheek.

"Digestible. Too much Cajun seasoning." She sniffed. Her English accent was a bit sharper, what with the spices stuffing up her sinuses. Never mind that she was squinting like she'd stared into the sun during a lunar eclipse, and that her nose was red from too much contact with tissues. "I believe I interrupted?"

Doc Arne tapped on his diagnostic tablet. "I was telling the patient, Ms. Lark—"

"Lark-Hale."

"Right. Ms. Lark-Hale."

"Mrs." Loredana crossed her arms. Her foot started tapping.

Doc Arne sighed. "Mercury's undergone a severe panic attack, in the middle of what's supposed to be his normal mission. He's got to be benched from Operations."

"Um, no," I said.

"Out of the question." Loredana shook her head.

"Things have been quiet, ma'am, except for these Syndax remnants." Garvey managed not to break his gaze as Loredana stared him down. Impressive feat, considering I'd seen her go head-to-head with zombies. Then again, so had he. "Wilhelmina and I can handle them if Mr. Hale needs recovery time."

"What I need is to A.) not be talked about like I'm not in the room, and B.) not be treated like an invalid because I had a panic attack." A twinge shot up my leg—the one that I had severed five months ago. It was drown or amputate. The prosthetic Liz designed held up nicely. Hadn't noticed it during the fight on the Promenade, not with it absorbing the pulsar stave's energy just like the suit did. "I'm good. We should be working on why those Syndax crazies were keen on sacrificing someone and how they were able to trigger a rip on their own, because news flash, I didn't see a portal gun on anybody besides Garvey."

"That is what Elizabeth is attempting to ascertain. I came to escort you to Tracking." Loredana offered her arm.

"Delightful." My English accent was terrible, but I grinned at my concerned infirmary audience, looped my arm through hers, and off we went.

Our steps carried us about thirty feet down the curved corridors of the base when Loredana murmured, "How are you, really?"

"Shaken."

"Not stirred?"

I chuckled. "You've definitely spent too much time with me."

"I believe that is part of the vow, 'in sickness and in health,' Mercury. Please. Be frank."

The word conjured up images of a grizzled, bearded, George Clooney lookalike piloting an armored mech against Syndax warriors. I shook my head. "It freaked me out, no joke. I'm surprised it didn't happen sooner, but then again, I haven't been in the water since. No time for a beach vacation."

"Prior to that, you reported no ill effects from your experience."

The prosthetic leg had more of a *clump* to it than my natural appendage, less meaty, more plastic and metal. "Yeah, nothing to report."

"That isn't what I meant. In the months since, there had been few moments that have not gone interrupted by threats from within and without this dimension. The strain of that work and the pandemic at large has, I believe, affected us all. Hence the overly attentive nature of your comrades."

"Not like we haven't had any breaks." My lips brushed her neck. Loredana snorted and goosed me in revenge. We rounded a corner, veering between two brawny guys from Security. They nodded. No sign of having noticed our public display of affection.

"Yes, quite." Her cheeks grew redder. "We have

had almost a year of overall unrelenting threat. Given you've suffered more in the face of adversity than any of us, it's small wonder your incident didn't happen sooner."

Heck of a vote of confidence. "Let's focus on Liz's research, okay? Then we can discuss whether or not I should have a wellness day."

"Dismiss my concerns all you want. Your mental well-being is no joking matter."

She entered the doorway to Tracking a few steps ahead, before I could zing her in response. Hmm. Probably best not to. We'd only been married a few months, but I was getting better at reading her moods—as I'm sure she was at reading mine. So even though she'd picked up on me being touchy about the whole freaking out when underwater thing, I'd figured out when I'd needled her enough, she got angry instead of mildly perturbed. The lift of her chin, the thin line of her mouth, the resolute gaze …

All signs I'd fouled up.

"Hey. I'm not dismissing anything. This rattled me, and I don't know how to deal with it –or if I should." I held out my hand. "I'm sorry."

She considered the gesture out of the corner of her eye for so long I thought she was trying to turn it to stone. Finally, her expression softened enough for a smile to curve the corners of her mouth. She took my hand. "I know. Apology accepted."

"Aww." Elizabeth Stojan was seated at the center console in Tracking, pink Converse sneakers propped on a desk. She wore black leggings and a long, yellow shirt under a denim jacket. Short spiky hair glowed as pink as the shoes under the fluorescent lights overhead. Another three people were scattered at their computers, muttering to each other from six feet away about whatever it was the data told them. Blinking indicators appeared on a map of California, with a box drawn around San Camillo and the northern coast.

What was that smell? Hand sanitizer, I guessed, with a touch of bleach. Tracking had never been cleaner.

"Good news, Liz?" I nudged her shoes over as I sat on the edge of the desk.

"You guys are so cute! I mean, that is good news, but the better news is what I found on the Syndax mercenaries before you turned them over to the feds." She cracked her knuckles and, waving her hands like she was gonna pull a rabbit out of a hat, tapped her console's screen.

The creature in the middle image looked as big as my hand, with gnarled, spindly legs. Its body was shaped like a tick, only with a robotic design. Something artificial, yet with natural elements—or vice versa.

"They had a symmachite on their persons," Loredana said. "Remarkable."

"Okay, but not just one. We took their armor to the lab because of the fluctuating tachyon readings we kept seeing, just like the ones that pointed us to the Promenade in the first place. Picked seven of these little guys off and quarantined them. They collapsed into their component molecules not long after we got them separated."

"So, Syndax left us samples." I squinted at the image. "And they're dead? No chance of leaking out and infecting anyone to the point of being brainwashed?"

"No way. Don't be silly. Crux's sword is locked away in deep storage, nowhere near the lab."

"That's great, really." I had no desire to repeat the exhausting battles I'd waged against Airfoil, my brother, and even Ramos when they were mind-controlled by the microscopic swarm.

Speaking of which …

"Correct me if I'm mistaken, Elizabeth, but when we last encountered these creatures, they operated as part of a great mass." Loredana stepped toward the map at the front of the room. "What is the likelihood they reappeared in similar numbers this time?"

"Small. I mean, really small. Smaller than them." Liz giggled. "But, okay, I ran the numbers through Cyril, and he thinks there must have been two more."

"Never gonna argue with your supercomputer when he makes up his mind, but only nine symmachites?" I raised an eyebrow. "You could probably fit them all on a pinhead. Or the tip of the pin."

"What? Oh. The magnification." Liz's shoes dropped to the floor. They squealed as she turned in her chair. She tapped commands into her console. Numbers appeared in the upper right-hand corner.

Loredana's eyebrows lifted, her equivalent of a burst of profanity.

"That's—you're kidding. Ten inches?" I grimaced. "I would have noticed a creepy cyber-spider the size of a dinner plate."

"Maybe, if it hadn't been tucked into the guy's vest. The astral fiend drained the soldier."

"Burns on his hand?"

Liz shook her head.

"Yeah. I heard the leader of the band tell someone else to open the rift. Guess he wasn't bluffing."

"And no, I don't know yet how exactly the spider-thing can do that. Manipulate a developing rip, I mean. Still working on it." Liz wrinkled her nose. "I'd love to have a live one."

"You did say there were two more, whereabouts currently unknown." Loredana spoke over her shoulder, her attention refocused on the map.

"That's what we've determined. Now, okay, so we have a couple tachyon hotspots that have popped up, and sure, we get a lot of those that never develop into anything." Liz swiped a new graphic onto her screen. The giant map in front of Loredana expanded to include North America, plus the Caribbean. Purple diamonds flashed in sixteen locations. "The Interstice is constantly bumping up against our dimension. Most times you won't see more than Two or Three on the old quality scale we use to classify those emissions."

I nodded. Forecasting would always help narrow it down. Before Marigold Yen, the former head of that department and dreamer of prescient dreams, turned out to be the villain intent on merging our sunny dimension full of humans with the stormy one full of astral fiends who liked to dine on said humans. "So, what does our new Forecasting chief have to say about this latest development?"

Liz chewed her lip. "She, um, won't tell me."

Loredana sighed. "I can see I shall have to resend my memo on inter-departmental cooperation."

"No, it's not—Ms. Pathkiller's keeping it to herself. I mean, she won't tell me or anyone else in Forecasting no matter how nicely I ask and I can be *really nice* because I even brought her coffee—!"

"Liz." I made a rolling motion with my hands.

"Sure. She says she'll only tell the operative."

I blew out a breath. "Well, we've got a boxful of those these days, but she probably means me."

Liz nodded.

"It is imperative we obtain a more precise location for these two escaped symmachites." Loredana and I rejoined Liz at her desk. "The damage they could cause running amok in their present enlarged state, I don't want to imagine, but it would be a far greater catastrophe should Syndax remnants recapture them."

"No kidding. But where'd they get them? You think somebody escaped our notice when Serena used her mercs and the symmachites to attack the base?" I sifted through my memories for the hazy recollection of San Camillo Police Department's monster squad—don't get me started on their acronym—hauling the guys we'd captured away to be federally imprisoned. "Something tells me no one was counting heads."

"Quite. I suspect that may have been the case. I'll inquire with Intelligence. Delia should be able to assist in this matter."

Right. Cordelia Keyes. Loredana's school gal pal, recently shown up at our wedding, and vanished just as soon. "Where's she stationed?"

"Around and about." Loredana touched my shoulder. "We should get you to Edith as soon as we can."

Oh, great. A Forecasting dream session. I was never fond of those, even though Marigold had been as sweet as a guy could hope for. She and her husband Winston Yen had been a rare couple on my tiny list of friends.

Now Marigold was dead, absorbed into the supernatural monstrosity of the Whisperer, combined with Alexander Arkwright, the former CEO and villain boss of Syndax Multinational. Winston was locked in a supermax prison upstate for the next bazillion years.

I was sure glad my list of friends and allies had grown in the past six months. Otherwise the expanding roster of bad people seeking to destroy, distort, or otherwise foul up Earth was growing depressingly fast.

"Thanks for the briefing, Liz." I held out my hand as Loredana and I walked for the door.

Liz high-fived my palm with a resounding *smack*. "I'll get those possible coordinates locked down. Oh! And I bet we can come up with something fun in the lab to help you capture the cyber-spiders. Maybe if I rerouted the particle flow on the cold gun you used against the astral fury ..."

Her voice faded into a constant stream of self-conversation as we turned down the corridor. I nudged Loredana. "You know, I don't need an escort this time."

"I never thought you did."

"Sure." I grinned. "Is that why you're still walking with me?"

Loredana frowned. "Edith—Ms. Pathkiller—Her talents are as of yet untested."

"The rest of Procyon didn't think so. That's why they had her hidden away in Middle of Nowhere, Nevada, claiming she was just some flunky running a secret outpost."

"True."

"And you did hire her."

"That is also true, though Mr. Alvarez, being the manager, signed the paperwork."

Ack. Paperwork. "She hasn't brought back Marigold's disclaimer forms, has she?"

"Please." Loredana stopped. She drew me in for a hug. "I am worried for you."

"Hey. I'll be all right." We held on to each other

as long as she needed. Not sure how many seconds or minutes, but since no one bothered us to get to Forecasting faster, I figured we weren't missed. "I get it. You don't trust her."

"I am trying. But after Marigold Yen—"

"Forget her. Edie fought with us. She's protected Procyon." I placed a hand on her cheek. "Tell you what—why don't you wait outside her office? Then you can deal with anything weird right away."

Loredana smirked. "How kind of you to give me a directive that is, in fact, what I planned to do."

"I'm *that good.*" I tapped the side of my head.

The Forecasting office was behind a metal door decorated with puke green peeling paint and a black sign announcing its name.

"Is there anything you need?" Loredana squeezed my hand.

"Yes. Absolutely." I looked her directly in the eyes. Keeping a straight face was one of the hardest things I'd ever done in my life. "The half-eaten stick of pepperoni from the break room fridge."

She swatted at me, but I dodged it. "The one bearing a Sticky Note proclaiming dismemberment for whoever steals your leftovers?"

I batted my eyelashes.

Loredana laughed. "I'd be happy to, assuming Garvey hasn't eaten it again."

"Garvey," I muttered. "My new nemesis."

I knocked on the door. Loredana started down the corridor for the break room, which was a few dozen yards to the left and around a bend. "Oh, and hey! We should probably consider heading home and getting some sleep soon. Before daylight. I hear it's a good practice."

"We can certainly do that, though, since it's been a while, I'd rather we exercised instead." She disappeared around the corner, that sly smile in place again.

Exercise. I grinned like a big goofball.

Have to say. I loved being married.

CHAPTER THREE

S pace wasn't unlimited in a former missile silo. Heck, we'd used the biggest square footage for a cylindrical parking garage. Everybody made use of what was available. Tracking, the lab, and the infirmary got priority. Eventually, crews would finish construction of the new offices on Bay Avenue, where Procyon had lived before the Hedron of Orbits destroyed it this fall.

But for the moment, Forecasting was stuck in a closet.

Okay, that's an exaggeration. The room was a decent size, probably thirty feet on each side. Once you packed in steel racks containing jug after jug of water, though, there wasn't a lot of wiggle room.

The steel door clanked shut behind me. I fidgeted with my sleeve. When Marigold ran Forecasting, it was in a softly lit office of soothing pastels and twenty shades of white, a serene, quiet space.

Edie's version was quiet, all right. Like a cemetery.

I walked down the center aisle, catching glimpses of my warped reflection in the water jugs. Hundreds of me, like my own Muppet fan club. Creepy.

There was a single chair set in one of two pools of amber light. I sat on the leather cushion. Wooden legs creaked.

Edith Pathkiller was already seated in an identical chair, facing me, eight feet away. Good social distancing, I noted.

Edie was a thirty-something woman, Native American, with black hair dangling clear to her waist, tied in a thick braid and coppery skin. Streaks of silver touched her temples. Two gold earring loops on each lobe and a tiny wolf piercing in her nose.

"So," I said. "Fun fact. I found out you're Cherokee."

"Mostly." When she spoke, it reminded me of hearing a breeze brushing through a forest. But it was also as commanding as a teacher's, if a teacher wore red and white flannel sleeveless shirts, with blue jeans that had lost their knees. "Are you going to recite my bloodlines? There's no extra credit."

My smile faded. Did she *know* I was thinking the teacher reference?

"Tell me what you see." She leaned forward, her elbows resting on her thighs, palms held up.

"Um ..." I scratched the back of my neck. "Nice manicure, Edie?"

"Edith. And, no."

"Right. Sorry."

She frowned. "Your role won't progress if you can't open your mind to the wider world, Mercury. There's so much possibility beyond what we perceive with our five senses."

"Okay. I kinda knew that, already, what with being born in another dimension—and getting married there. Besides, you're the Forecaster. We take our direction from you about hints of the other worlds. Tachyon tracking can only get us so far."

"The gift I possess isn't one that's locked away from other people. You have to open yourself to the perception of time. Time isn't sitting still." She tapped the wooden arm of the chair. "Unlike us. The past, the present, the future … They're in motion. We've already traveled to the future, if you consider it."

"I missed the trip."

"No. Time wandered away while we were talking. You, me, the world, everyone and everything in it, is seconds older. The past of two minutes ago is gone."

I nodded, as if I could understand what she was talking about. My questions and answers toward the more concrete—as in, where was the monster and how fast could I slay it. But I wasn't about to push Edie on the matter. This was her domain.

"Oklahoma." She reached for a tablet perched on the shelf to her right, which I realized was missing a few water jugs. A potted cactus stood under a tiny lamp, soaking in a light so brilliant I imagined I could feel the heat.

"Huh?" I thought she'd sneezed.

"It's a state. In America."

Yeesh. Thought I was the king of sarcasm. "Yeah, pretty sure I've flown over it."

"That's your first destination."

"First."

Edie swiped through the table. She met my eyes with a stare that I found at once beautiful and disconcerting. "What's your problem, Operative?"

"I don't have a problem." I shifted in my chair. One of the legs squeaked against the concrete floor. "We've fought against the same enemies. Means we're on the same side."

"Is that why Loredana is waiting outside my door for you to finish this session?"

"Okay, how about you cut out the mind-reading? Sure, she's out there. You're the new person. And given the reputation of the last person to hold your job, probably worth it to check in on you discreetly. But not as discreetly as we'd tried."

Edie chuckled. "I don't fault you at all. It's her perfume, by the way. Not mind-reading. You've carried more of her scent on you than before."

My cheeks burned. "Oh. Right."

"Here." Edie turned the tablet so I could see a Google map glowing in the dim light. I was expecting a detailed technical readout like the ones that would come across my phone from Loredana or Liz, courtesy of tracking's geek team and their petabytes of available data.

No such thing. Liz had drawn a yellow circle

around a suburban neighborhood. Gated community, surrounded by trees and empty land. Couple bodies of water.

Cold splashed on me like I'd been dumped in the bay again. Sweat beaded my upper lip. Easy, Mercury. Freaking out every time I saw a picture of a pond was not going to help me conquer my newfound phobia. "Thanks."

"You're welcome."

Something she said echoed from the back of my mind. "First?"

"Yes. First destination."

"There's more than one? Have the cyber-spiders split up?" The name was growing on me, I realized. Nice work, Liz.

Edie gazed at me. "I've had—impressions. Hints. Nothing substantial beyond Oklahoma. But there's something more. It won't come to me yet."

"When will you know more?"

"When it's ready to reveal itself."

I rolled my eyes. "The dream or the cyber-spider?"

"There's no difference. We walk around like our presence doesn't leave an imprint on the fabric of space and time, like we move through this world without consequence even though parts of us are from somewhere else." She leaned back in her chair and, with a motion so smooth I admired how she didn't fall from her chair, crossed her legs underneath herself. She was barefoot. Hadn't noticed earlier.

"Look, maybe you could give me something more

to go on." I jerked a thumb at the door. "Loredana's a 'give me the coordinates, please' kind of person, and I gotta say, that approach works for me."

"Do you really want to see?"

I shrugged.

She held out her right hand, fingers splayed. There was an onyx band on the pinky. The violet tattoo of a pawprint on her right shoulder glistened in the lamplight.

High … Five? I brought my hand toward hers. Go team!

She grasped it, fingers intertwining with mine. Her grip was so strong it caught me off balance and pulled my off the cushion. Knees? Meet concrete floor.

"*See.*"

Edie's voice was two octaves lower and overlapped with what sounded like a full chorus. Her eyes took on a purple tinge and went flashlight-white, LED bulbs of flesh, a lot like Bowen Cord's when he threw ice magic through the air. He's an ice-summoner … Never mind, long story.

As for me …

I left the Forecasting room, shot through concrete and dirt and pine trees like they weren't in my way, and hurtled through a blurred sky.

I yelled without sound. No wind buffeting me, either. No sensation. Not until I landed on the color-smeared grass of a tiny island in the middle of a lake with the force of a bomb's shockwave. Mud stained my hands. Rain drenched my clothes.

There was a chest. Genuine treasure chest. It rattled. Something or somethings scraped at the inside, clawing for a way out.

Spindly legs of shimmering metal and mottled purple-gray scales crawled over its lid …

I gasped.

Back in Forecasting. Not wet. Not muddy. But breathing as if I'd run a marathon—or, you know, flown thousands of miles round trip in seconds.

"Any questions?" Edie wiped her palm against her jeans, gaze never leaving mine, even as the glow faded from her eyes.

Are you kidding? "Nope. I'm good."

"Then sign here." She swiped across the tablet and set it on my lap. Then she walked off into the recesses of the room and opened another door. Golden light flooded in. Might have been cozy office furniture beyond that rectangle, too, but she shut the door so fast my eyes hurt when darkness returned.

I glanced down at the tablet. A release statement readying me for in the field action.

"Paperwork," I muttered.

Once we had the location plugged in for the cyber-spider, there wasn't much we could do except wait for Liz to get her latest lab project completed. Whatever she had in mind for the ice gun we'd used to stop a giant mutated astral fiend from burning down San Camillo and its environs wasn't an hour-long project.

It meant Loredana and I could go home for the night.

I made the drive in record time. I mean, how hard was it, when there was zero traffic? The governor of California had issued his shelter in place order with the coronavirus spreading throughout the state. How Procyon got itself exempted, I wasn't about to ask, but I felt like I should wave at any passing car, just for solidarity's sake.

Home was Loredana's Tabb Terrace condo. We were still in the market for a new place we could call ours, but with Procyon business shunting our search efforts aside, we'd agreed on her place as the better of the two locations to inhabit on our joint incomes. Besides, it was way easier for me to adapt to Loredana's condo than it was for her to settle into my loft. My old place would have needed a *lot* of work. Aside from the uniformity of color—pretty sure the painter had used every variation of white available from the hardware store—it was just a much more relaxing place.

Besides, she hadn't fussed at all about the addition of a framed *Cowboy Bebop* poster. It hung bold red right next to signed headshots of Christopher Eccleston and Matt Smith.

None of which I was actually looking at when the doorbell rang at seven the next morning.

I groaned and rolled over. Slapped at my phone twice before I could get the screen started. Then had to turn it right side up. My ear landed in a damp patch on my pillow. Drool. Classy. I rubbed at the corner of my mouth with my hand.

"You have my permission to shoot the offender," Loredana murmured.

"Six fifty-six." I slumped back against the pillow. "Not getting up."

Loredana poked my bare ribs. "It is your turn. I answered the phone last time. You said, and I quote, 'I totally owe you.'"

I winced. Yeah, yeah, I had.

The doorbell rang again. Then the jerk knocked.

"New least favorite person." I whipped aside the sheets and staggered from the bedroom.

Hmm. I stopped by the mirror. Looking good, muscles and all, but probably shouldn't answer the door in only black boxers. I snagged a Procyon T-shirt off the dresser and scooted out, phone in hand.

I dialed up some Aerosmith and let it blast from the speakers, giving me the opportunity for an awesome Tom Cruise *Risky Business* slide down the short corridor. I peeked through the door's eyehole.

"You've got to be kidding me," I muttered.

I swung the door open. Agent Hudson Bowe, Department of Homeland Security, filled the entrance, liked he'd been poured into too small a container. Dude was the size of two football players, looking like a younger, blond version of Santa Claus who'd retired from the NFL and decided to live out the rest of his days on a ranch instead of slinging toys around the globe. The black blazer was the only thing formal about his attire. Rumpled white shirt pinstriped with green, blue jeans, cowboy boots …

"You can take the boy out of Montana but not the Montana out of the boy, eh, Bowe?" I leaned against the frame. "What's up?"

"You, at Too Early a.m." He smirked and hooked his thumbs in his jeans pockets. The motion pushed his jacket back far enough I could see the shiny Homeland badge hanging from one pocket and the pistol dangling from a leather holster on the other side. "Morning, Mercury. How's married life treating you?"

"It's Mark Hale. Says so on my driver's license."

"Sure does. And on all your other paperwork—of which there's very, very little. I'm not here to play games. Tell me about that ruckus at the Promenade."

"Ruckus? Haven't been to a ruckus in a while." I leaned back into the condo. "Hey, Loredana! When was the last time I took you to a ruckus?"

"Somewhere around your bachelor party," came the bemused reply.

"See?" I grinned. "No ruckus."

Bowe took a step forward. I sidestepped and blocked his passage. Bowe pointed. "Mind if I sit a spell?"

"Yeah, I do. Last time I extended hospitality to a federal agent, she wound up betraying all of us to a madman from another dimension." I snapped my fingers. "Oh, by the way, if you're looking for Serena Cyr, Loredana shot her and she got dumped into the

Interstice. Not that you don't already know all that."

"You got a real smart mouth, you know that, Mercury?" Bowe snapped. Ah. Hit a nerve, did I? "Would've been nice if you'd tipped off Homeland so we could arrest her before she caused more trouble."

"I didn't have time to be put on hold fifty times trying to call, what, your anti-terror hotline?" I snorted. "Face it, Bowe—you should stick to the run-of-the-mill terrorists. Leave the otherworldly threats to the pros."

"That's a negative. You're forgetting, Syndax Multinational operated on U.S. soil for years before they revealed their true selves. Homeland's made their eradication a priority. *My* priority." He pointed at me. "Which is why I'm here. To remind you to steer clear of them."

"Steer clear. That's a great idea. I'll let them kill innocent people and leave the corpses for you to clean up, right?" I shook my head. "Fat chance, Bowe. Look: Clearly, we work the best when I leave presents via our SCPD delivery people. Why can't you just be happy and take credit when I drop them off at your figurative doorstep?"

"Because you're rogue. I don't care how much pull you have elsewhere in the federal government—"

"It's a lot," I stage whispered.

"—There's still proper channels for getting these things done. Can't believe I'm 'bout to say this, but I don't got tolerance for cowboys." He chuckled. "At least, not your variety."

"That a racial comment?"

"I mean vigilantes." Bowe sighed. "Don't get all bent out of shape. Procyon's actions leak out to the public more and more every day. Serena's dropped more intel from both our organization's than either's comfortable with."

"Let me try some active listening, Bowe—I hear you saying you're going after Syndax and you want me to stay out the way." I spread my arms and shrugged. "Fair enough?"

"Right on target." Bowe dug a tiny pocketknife from his jacket and went to work on his canines like he had raw meat lodged in there. Who knows? Maybe he'd already eaten a steak. Or a whole cow. "'Cause if you are snooping around outside of your jurisdiction, I'll shut you down and lock you up until people with more say than either of us can clean up the mess. No more vigilantism for you."

"Sounds like a great idea. Except when I say great, I mean stupid." I lifted my chin. "Here's a better one—when the monsters show up again, and they will, whether it's here or elsewhere, you either stay out of my way or lend support fire to cut them down. Better yet, just get back in your fedmobile and watch it on YouTube."

Bowe chuckled again. Didn't sound happy, really. Kind of made me think of a lion or a bear, grumbling on a pleasantly full belly. The grin he had could have been full of fangs, too, if he'd been an astral fiend. "Syndax is a national security matter, so stay in town, Mercury. No one's supposed to be traveling anywhere these days, so it shouldn't be a stretch. If you don't, keep in mind Homeland and I might not be far behind. Make sure to check your rear-view mirror, all right?"

He sauntered down the hall, like he had nowhere to go, whistling a tune I couldn't place but might have pinpointed if I'd tuned in to country radio.

Well. That was fun. Nothing like getting threatened by a federal agent with an independent task force hunting the same ghostly remnants of an organization Procyon was trying to take down.

"A lovely chat, no doubt." Loredana's voice startled me enough I dropped my phone.

Her hand shot out and caught it. Between the white T-shirt with the red word "Prickly" in the center and the green pajama pants covered with cartoony white hedgehogs, she looked like a college gal who didn't want to get up for class—except she already acted more awake than me. Without coffee. Which should have been illegal.

"Oh, you know Homeland. Always in the neighborhood to make sure we're doing okay."

"Their ... interest in this matter with Syndax doesn't change our operational plans."

"Heck no." I looped an arm around her shoulders. "Assuming Alvarez doesn't wring his hands about this social call."

"One assumes I intend to inform him." Loredana tucked my phone back into my waiting fingers. "We should get breakfast and return to Procyon as soon as we can."

"After coffee." I rubbed my eyes. "Lots of coffee."

"I concur."

CHAPTER FOUR

Liz was ready for us before noon. Which gave us plenty of time to talk to Alvarez about our upcoming travel plans.

He was, understandably, perturbed. Because "perturbed" was his default mode.

"I've spent all morning on conference calls with the directors of Homeland Security and the FBI." Alvarez walked with us to the lab, two steps ahead. Quite the feat, considering he was shorter-legged than both of us. He didn't fit in with the rest of the Procyon crew working in the base's warren of corridors. A silver-gray suit with black shirt and red tie weren't the dress code for people either in the lab coats of research or medical staff, the black polos of Security, or the varied civilian garb of Tracking. "The only highlight you need to know is that they're both so busy sniping at each other's heels that they're not paying too close attention to our activities."

"I would think we prefer it so," Loredana said.

Alvarez stopped up short and glared up at us. He wasn't a rolly-poly guy, but thickset, with wavy black hair and a goatee befitting the coolest pirate ever. I wondered if he'd ever wrestled, in high school or college. He walked like a guy who could take care of himself in a rough neighborhood. "I'd prefer it if Homeland agents didn't have to make early morning visits to my personnel."

I scratched the back of my neck. Loredana stared resolutely ahead.

"But that doesn't mean I'm going to allow a desk-bound bureaucrat in D.C. to dictate our next moves. If this creature is in fact loose and has somehow manifested itself in Midwest town a thousand miles away, it has to be stopped."

"Shall I interpret your comments as authorization to proceed with our mission?" Loredana could have been asking for a wine list at an elegant restaurant. Me? I bounced on my toes like a kid who found out tomorrow was a snow day—and believe me, I couldn't remember the last time we'd had one in California.

"Interpret my response as acknowledgement that you need time off from your standard duties." Alvarez frowned. "As soon as we get into our new office, we'll be putting proper procedures back into place, but as it is, I don't have time to micromanage Operations."

"Bummer," I muttered. "Wouldn't want to deprive you of life's joys."

"I don't need your glib attitude, Hale. Make sure

you two come back alive. There's a board meeting next week, and Loredana needs to on Zoom for it, away from danger."

"I will convey my schedule to the next monster we encounter." Loredana lifted an eyebrow. "If you'll excuse us …"

Alvarez was already turning the next corner, speaking in rapid-fire Spanish into his phone. Couldn't make out all the words—my translating suffers when Google isn't involved—but somebody was behind on the armor-plated glass being secretly installed in the new office building.

As long as headquarters could withstand future gravity-distorting attacks that could crush entire structures, I was happy with that.

Liz's lab had the least redecorating since our arrival at the silo. Not much there besides concrete walls, boxes of all shapes and sizes, tables covered with unidentifiable equipment. I knew she had a cleaner workspace somewhere else. She had to. No way she could have pieced together high-tech gear in what amounted to a dingy basement.

"Hey guys!" Grease stains marred her cheeks. Liz waved us over to where the ice gun used to be mounted. Good-bye three-foot-long cannon that harnessed the pulsar stave's energy to produce intense cold. Hello short, stubby … Thing. It reminded me of half a toaster, turned on its end, with a narrow, rectangular slit for a muzzle.

"That's kinda shrimpy," I said.

Loredana prodded me. "Don't be rude."

"What? It is."

Liz waved her hand like she was wafting a bad smell. "It's okay, Ms. Lark. He'll like it anyway. It's a further modification of what started out as the portal device Gary DeBarthe created, and actually gets back to its roots. Nobody's gonna freeze anything with this puppy! It's a stasis initiator."

"Okay." I took it from her. There was a space where the grip should have been. "I plug the pulsar stave in here?"

"Yep. It works like the ice gun, in that respect, but when you aim it at an object, it kind of opens a rip."

"That—sounds bad."

"No, no, it's a tiny one." Liz made a pinching motion with her thumb and forefingers. She squinted through the space. "Maybe about this big. More than what's needed to disrupt space-time."

"Not gonna lie, still sounds bad."

Loredana pressed a finger to my lips and winked at me. "Let the poor woman finish. Elizabeth, this small rip's purpose I gather is to incapacitate a creature rather than simply obliterating it or returning it to the Interstice."

"Yes! Yes. I mean, we need to study one of these live, and even then, that's difficult under microscopic conditions. Having a cyber-spider that we could dissect?" Liz clapped her hands together. "So much fun!"

I powered up the pulsar stave and inserted it into

the energy port. A hum built to the level of a nearby, gigantic mosquito. "Don't suppose you've got a target for me?"

"Try the cardboard box."

"Which one?" But I picked out a half-open, empty container laying on its. I pressed the trigger plate in front of the stave.

There was a whip-crack of sound, a ripple of air, and a flash of purple light. A pale rainbow that seemed to be streaming in reverse struck out at the box, encasing it in a cloudy form. I could see multiple versions of the box—some brand new and sealed, other torn and crumpled. If I shifted my stance, the image changed.

"See? Stasis!" Liz slapped my arm.

"Great. But how do we move the object or target or whatever once it's frozen like that?" I tipped the gun onto my shoulder. "Because I'm not keen on putting my hands into a mini-rip."

"That's what these are for." She gave Loredana a pair of gloves with sleeves that reached up to the elbow. I could have sworn she'd cut them off my suit, except they were school bus yellow patterned with jagged black lines. "I patterned them after the supersuit. I mean, not last night. It's been one of my side projects. They'll absorb and deflect tachyon particles, providing a shield between the person and the latent energies swarming around a rip. We've got a mobile container you guys can use, like a suitcase on wheels. It'll hold the cyber-spider for your return trip."

Loredana slid the gloves on over her hands. Had to say, it gave her a serious superhero vibe. "Thank you, Elizabeth. These shall do nicely."

"You bet!" She snapped her fingers. "Oh! I'll go get your container. He'll be handy."

"He?" I shook my head as she sprinted from the lab. "You know, if we cut the cyber-spider apart, we wouldn't have to worry about all this stuff. I bet it would even sublimate. Pile of goo, much?"

"That will not give us the answers we need. This is a new lifeform, one for which our experience with astral fiends leaves us unprepared. It is a danger that must be contained but not obliterated—at least, not until we determine the extent of its purposes."

"Fair enough." I removed the stave from its socket and twirled it, letting the alternating heat and cold seep into my fingers. Its energies had weird effects like that, depending on how it was being used. The thing felt like it had moods, at times.

Like when it had automatically purged my body of a symmachite infestation, preventing them from seizing control of me.

"But do me a favor," I said. "Let's keep their destruction an option."

"It always is," Loredana said.

Liz's suitcase turned out to be an automated container on two big wheels. It was circular itself, with a hatch that opened into a ceramic space. Pulsing orange lights surrounded its curve on the inside.

Outside, it was eggshell white with brass-colored panels.

It rolled up to me, halting a foot away from my shoe.

"Did you build us a droid?" I knelt and tapped on the unit's hatch.

"Nope. I wish! It's got a very rudimentary GPS system and sensing equipment. I've got a Bluetooth signal that will keep him following your phones." Liz knelt with me. "But it won't respond to voice commands or anything like that."

"He's similar to a car's hubcap," Loredana observed. "Or a wheel rolling free."

"Hub." I nodded. "Good enough name for me. Guess we'd better load up. I don't suppose we can convince Dominic to portal us to Oklahoma."

"Sadly, he's otherwise occupied. We shall take my airplane."

My disappointment at not having Dominic Zein use the Echo Watches to make our multi-state trip instantaneous vaporized as soon as Loredana said airplane. I grinned at my reflection in Hub's shiny flank. "Hear that? I call shotgun."

I hadn't ridden in Loredana's private jet since we'd fled San Camillo with Skipper—also known as Bowen Cord, a powerful magic summoner from yet another dimension—to Rampart, Colorado, in our first and only attempt to infiltrate Syndax. That had ended with us retrieving Gary DeBarthe, late of Procyon's Tracking department, only to get trapped in a Syndax compound with a bunch of corpse-fiend zombies. If it hadn't been for Dominic, who knows how long we would have been stuck.

But if I was gonna have to fly halfway across the country, I was happy to take the airborne equivalent of a Jaguar, leather seats and all—a Cirrus Vision Jet, a sleek, hot rod. The turbofan jet on its back screamed through a V-shaped tail as we pierced the clouds around San Camillo.

I napped clear through to Salt Lake City, dead to my surroundings until we touched down for a brief refueling—and restroom—stop. Talk about a ghost town. The place was near empty of fliers. The pandemic had gutted air travel, from what little news I'd absorbed on my phone. I nodded off again, just for a spell, because the Cirrus lifted into the air, bouncing through some mild turbulence.

"Back among the living, I hear." Loredana looked as relaxed as I felt, sunlight reflecting off aviator shades, leaned back in the pilot's chair.

"Don't you mean, you see?" I stretched my arms, which meant I could touch both sides of the cockpit. "'Cause I didn't hit the can while invisible in the supersuit."

"A joke, Mercury. Definitely 'hear.' Your snoring stopped."

"Wow."

Loredana tapped her headphones. "Through

these, too."

"Well, that's cheating if you keep the volume up."

She laughed. I loved that sound. "Here, I think you'll find this more diverting." She handed me her phone from beside her seat.

It was open to a Facebook post put up by a mom of two young boys. They lived in Whispering Pines, our destination suburb. She rambled about how blessed she was to have a doting husband, a wonderful family, full of love and snuggles and blah blah blah. I rolled my eyes. If this was Loredana's way to get me thinking about having a family, I had news for her—sickeningly sweet was *not* a motivator.

"Cute, I guess." I set the phone down. "Her kids' story about toy dinosaurs trying to eat them was fun. I'd read the book."

"The narrative is fascinating, because of its provenance to our assignment. It is from the same coordinates Elizabeth and Edith marked for us."

"Sure, but—"

"I have also gathered atmospheric data from the region, compiled over the past year. Whispering Pines has experienced particularly unsettled weather compared to surrounding communities."

"Okay." I squinted at her. "Don't like where this is going."

"Our roles require us to be open to the possibility of new and improbable phenomena," she said. "Procyon is built on such a principle."

Hadn't Edie said similar? The dream or vision

or whatever she'd shared with me flashed back into my head. The rain, the creepy chest, the island in the middle of a pond …

"Hang on." I re-read the Facebook post. "These kids—they claim they buried a weird chest with the dinos inside."

"Yes, I saw."

"Yeah, and so did I." A couple taps put me into the map Liz provided, on both our phones. I zoomed in and held it up, giving Loredana a clear view of a pond with an island at its center. The pond was big as a football field, surrounded by homes and trees on a loop road at the far end of the gated community. Whispering Pines had its own fishing dock, with tiny boats visible on the satellite image. "That island. When Edie linked me to her vision, I was there. Saw the chest. Got mud on me and everything."

"Remarkable." Loredana lifted her sunglasses for a better look. "I had hoped we would narrow the search field, but this—"

"This is freaky."

"Quite."

"I gotta say, this whole vision of me? Not a fan of a Forecaster being able to tap into my mind like that. Marigold never did."

"We have to reassess everything we thought we knew about how she did her job, in light of her betrayal."

I scratched the back of my neck. "Probably true. What's the plan for when we get there?"

"You tell me. You're the operative."

"You're the handler."

"In more ways than one, it seems." She smiled slyly. "I have the necessary credentials to bypass the gate guard. Once in the neighborhood, our objective should be the island immediately after dark."

"Got it. Should keep the questions to a minimum."

"From the residents, yes." Loredana peeked over the tops of her glasses. "Whereas our questions of this mystery, I'm afraid, might take longer to answer."

Whispering Pines' gate house was a small house-slash-box with broad windows, a nice fit with the wooden fence surrounding the entire neighborhood. A lone guard in simple black uniform glanced up from his cell phone, eyes widening at the silver rental sedan with tinted windows. Of course, I guessed he was more interested in Loredana's smile and her sapphire eyes as she peered over half-lowered shades. "Good evening."

"Uh, evening, folks." His voice was friendly, with a touch of anxiety at the edges. His badge read "Security," on a silver strip over his pocket. "Sorry, but this is a gated community."

"The gate tipped me off," I said cheerily from the passenger seat.

Loredana pinched my leg but said to the guard, "I think you'll find our credentials in order, Mr. ..."

"Hardt."

"Mr. Hardt. This is national security business."

She handed him a small folio, like a passport. It had a gray cover and no external markings I could see. But as soon as Hardt opened it, he stared open-mouthed.

"Centerfold in miniature?" I whispered.

"Kindly *shush*," Loredana said through gritted teeth.

"Yes, ma'am! I understand, ma'am." Hardt fumbled the folio but managed to only dump it in Loredana's lap. "We, ah, we'll keep this off the residents' radar. If anyone calls you in, I'll mention it's a local law enforcement drill."

"I appreciate your discretion."

The gate trundled open, and we drove in, taking the first right onto a road that ended near a sprawling park. There was more new playground equipment tucked in the clearing than I'd seen in one place.

The air outside was thick with moisture, humid enough for paper to mold in five seconds. I slung a backpack over my shoulder and lowered the brim of a black baseball cap. "Better hoof it from here, so the locals don't report on a strange car cruising by their homes."

"Agreed." Loredana's hair was secured under her cap. In our black jackets and olive-green fatigue pants, we didn't look like we were out for a stroll, but operational attire was operational attire.

I, for one, was glad for the extra garb as we passed modest two-story homes hemmed in by big oaks whose branches reached like astral fiend tentacles frozen against the evening sky, black silhouettes on a deep blue background. No stars out, but a crescent moon. Clouds crept in from the northwest. My phone said to expect rain.

The prospect made me shiver, and that had nothing to do with the temps dropping into the 40s. There was rain in Edie's vision, too …

"This way." Loredana slunk between a row of shrubs tall enough to swallow an adult. Hub rolled between us, his treaded wheels super quiet. If it weren't for the soft hum like a muted remote-control car, I'd have guessed he was still back in the airplane.

Lights were out in the houses on either side. Everyone was in bed, I guessed. In fact, most homes were dark.

I checked my watch. Ten fifteen.

We scooted through the trees on the sloping banks. The pond spread out like a mirror of the sky above. I craned my neck. Not long before the moon disappeared behind the clouds. "Once the moonlight's gone, we can paddle out."

"Excellent." Loredana removed a dark bundle from her backpack. She spread it out and yanked on a silver handle attached to a short cable. The inflatable raft flopped open and began expanding. She pieced together a paddle from the backpack. "We shall make quick work."

"As long as the stasis device doesn't make too much of a ruckus. That Hardt guy would probably call the cops on us if we shine that thing like a beacon—"

Light blinded me. I whipped the pulsar stave out, igniting its energies, and pivoted in my crouch so I was guarding Loredana.

"Who's there?" She had the heel of her hand on a holstered pistol.

A flurry of hissed whispers ended with a yelp, "Oz, no!" A dark shape hurtled at me, flashlight making those stupid blobs appear in my eyes when I looked away.

When I blinked through the afterimages, I was facing a kid wearing a Spider-man mask. "Okay, who are you? What are you looking for?"

A lot of interrogatory from a squeaky voice. "Kid, go home and stay in bed. Official business. As in, government." Sort of. I'd have to worry about lying to children later.

"Get the flashlight out of his face, Oz!" Another kid, this one taller and working on being in charge, pushed the littler one's hand down until the beam made a brilliant circle on the ground.

"Iggy, we gotta tell Mom and Dad! They're not supposed to be here!" Spider-child pointed toward the island. "Nobody's supposed to go out there!"

"Yeah, I know, but I think it's okay. Don't you know who it is?" The older kid looked up at me, eyes wide. He gestured at the pulsar stave. "It's Mercury Hale!"

CHAPTER FIVE

The first drops of rain spattered on my face and clinked where they hit the pulsar stave. I eyeballed this kid, the one who somehow thought he knew my name. I wasn't gonna tell him he was right. It was supposed to be a secret identity.

Not that I was super careful about that secret.

"Is that your weapon?" Iggy raised a hand toward the pulsar stave. "Wow."

"Hey! Look with your eyes." I yanked it away. "It's, ah, for illumination."

The shorter kid, tipped up his Spider-man mask, revealing Asian features. They argued like brothers. "If it's his weapon it'll burn your hands, Iggy."

"It's not burning his hand, Oz."

"Duh! It's *magic*."

"Children." Loredana put on the sweetest, most comforting smile I think I'd ever seen on her face, like a kindergarten teacher soothing nervous students on the first day of school. "It's quite late. You should be at home in bed, before your parents awake and find you gone. We wouldn't want to worry them."

Oz shook his head. "Dad sleeps through anything. Even monsters."

"No such thing as monsters." I deactivated the stave and slipped it into my jacket.

"Are so," Oz said.

"Shut *up*," Iggy hissed. "Mr. Hale, sir, we've seen the videos of you fighting. All those squid-things, and even zombies!"

"Iggy wants your autograph," Oz muttered. "And a hug."

Iggy sighed. I tried really hard not to laugh. The little brother reminded me of someone. Gee, wonder who?

"Look, guys, you can fake anything online. As in, Deep Fake. Slapping my head on a body from a video game is no big deal." I waved my hand, Obi-wan style. "And when we're talking about monsters—"

"They're real," Iggy said. "We know."

"We captured them!" Oz grabbed a branch from the ground and swung it at the nearest tree. "Epic battle! They didn't stand a chance!"

"It wasn't that easy, okay? We had to trick them with their food. That was the only way we could lock them up in the chest."

"The chest."

"Yeah. The big trunk that came from Mr. Chesterson's house."

I didn't know what to say to that. If I was just

going on the Facebook post Loredana had showed me, I'd say the kids had hyperactive imaginations. But coupled with Edie's shared vision, and the reality if the strangeness that came part and parcel with the Interstice …

"You're speaking of the dinosaurs, of course," Loredana said.

"They came to life and tried to eat us—tried to eat everyone!" Oz jabbed his stick into the tree. The stick snapped against the bark. "And we defeated them!"

"We were lucky," Iggy said. "If our friends hadn't helped us, I don't know if we could have stopped them. You need a good team when you're fighting monsters, right, Mr. Hale? I saw you with them—Airfoil! And the man who could vanish and reappear."

I scratched under the back of my cap. He wasn't wrong. "Okay. Let's assume you're telling the truth."

Oz muttered something I couldn't hear, that might have included the word "stupid," but Iggy elbowed him, eliciting and "Ow!" and a return smack.

"That's enough." Loredana separated them at either end of her arms.

"The chest. It's on the island. Where?" I asked.

"Um …" Iggy shuffled his shoes. "I don't know. Not actually. Todd Sterns put it out there, because no one goes out on the pond."

Oz pointed at the raft. "No boats allowed."

"Sure. Rules are rules, but this is a secret mission." I dropped my volume for the last two words. "Top secret. There's a new monster. Not a big one. Probably just as dangerous as the big ones, though. We're here to capture it."

"One of the dinos?" Iggy asked.

"Not precisely," Loredana said. "However, we believe it has been drawn to the phenomena which makes the chest a haven for your … Re-animated toys."

"We could help you find it!" Iggy headed for the raft, standing himself at the front like he was gonna George Washington across the Delaware.

"Iggy! If we go out on the pond, Dad's gonna kill us." Oz pulled on his brother's arm, but the older kid wouldn't budge.

"Easy, guys. This is too dangerous. We can't take you there." I raised a finger. "What I need, though, is a pair of lookouts. Someone who can signal us with a flashlight if anyone comes around while we're capturing the monster. You guys up to it?"

"Sure! We've got our flashlight."

"Like the bat-signal!" Oz snapped on the beam. I got a face full of bright light.

"Yeah. I noticed."

Loredana reached out and patted Iggy on the cheek. "There's a good lad. Thank you for your service."

Kinda hard to tell in the dark, with only a flashlight between the four of us, but I was pretty sure the kid was blushing. He sure seemed to have a lot more color in his cheeks.

Loredana and I pushed the inflatable raft out onto the pond, its bottom rustling over the grass. Hub rolled right over the edge, settling into the center. She managed to board with the grace of an equestrian mounting her horse. Me? I belly-crawled in but held the sides so we didn't get swamped.

We paddled toward the island as the skies opened. Those drips? They became a full-fledged downpour. The ballcaps were no good, except to keep me from wiping my eyes every five seconds. Otherwise they soaked up water.

Loredana had her phone perched on her pant leg, secured by a Velcro strap. It emitted tiny but sharp beeps. A red light flickered on its top edge.

"Tachyon emissions are increasing." She had to almost shout to be heard over the hiss of the rain. "Come around to the southeast side of the island."

"Sure." I spat rain. "How about you navigate, and I paddle? Since you've got the GPS and the tachyon dowser, to boot."

Loredana turned the phone on its side and adjusted the slender, black oval with a white triple outline attached to the back. Gold lights flickered in a triple curve along the edge. "It's holding up well despite being nearly as waterlogged as we are."

"Super." I could see the dark lump of the island, looming like a slumbering fiend. "Next mission or quest or whatever we take, we go somewhere drier. Winnemucca, Nevada, was nice and arid."

"I shall consider that change to our itinerary after

we secure the creature."

The raft bumped against the island. Not a big patch of land. With the pond football field-sized, there wasn't room for a huge sprawling mass. You could park a half dozen SUVs on it and have room for a romantic couple to stroll the edges, but that was it.

I pulled the raft up as Loredana disembarked. She ducked branches from the handful of trees and squeezed between tightly packed shrubs. Hub trundled in her wake, guided by the tracking systems in the phone. "Any luck?"

"Not as such. The signal is strong, and near, however ..."

I didn't like it when she stopped talking mid-sentence. I found her near a gash in the shrubs. A big gash. Like something had smashed through it.

"The chest was here." Loredana traced her finger around an imprint where the grass had been flattened—a large rectangle. "Up until less than twenty-four hours ago."

"It's rainy here. You mentioned the weather being lousier than usual." There was a long streak through the gash, down a shallow slope to the waterline. I brushed through the branches, letting them scratch my face and jacket so I didn't ruin the path with my boots. "Maybe the chest slipped along?"

Even as I said it, the theory didn't make sense. Iggy and Oz described the chest as being large enough to sit on top of and fit a boatload of toy dinosaurs. No way something that heavy would have slid even on the slickest, wet patch of grass. The slope wasn't steep enough for rain and gravity to do the trick.

Loredana's shoulder pressed against mine. "It did move this way. And I do believe you've found its resting place."

"Yeah. Lucky me." The flattened grass and streaked mud ended at a one-foot drop-off, where the island's waterline had eroded along a five-yard patch. Something had gone over the edge. "How deep you think it is?"

"Impossible to tell."

I extended one of the boat paddles to its max length and poked it down as far as it would go. "Three feet plus. Can't hit anything."

Loredana held her phone and its attached tachyon dowser above the drop-off. The red light blinked so fast it was almost a continuous pulse. "However deep the pond's bottom, the spider—and one assumes, the chest—is down there."

My guts shuddered. There was only one way to get it back up here and heading back into town to rent a tow truck wasn't that way. I sat on top of Hub, who thankfully didn't roll away and leave me cheeks-first in a patch of mud. Unlacing boots in pouring rain wasn't the way I wanted to spend a night out with my wife, but I got them off and stowed my socks inside one. Better keep them dry. I stripped out of the jacket and the shirt, too, because I didn't want every article of clothing soaking wet.

"Be back in a sec." I winked at Loredana—

because I needed the bravado waaaay more than she did—and jumped in.

"Mercu—!"

The tremendous splash and rumble of water in my ears cut off the rest of her cry. I powered the pulsar stave, which made for a handy underwater light source.

Would have been even better if there wasn't so much silt I could only see a couple feet beyond my nose.

The pond was deeper than I expected. I felt like I sank for minutes until my toes touched the top of something solid and slimy. I bent over, shining the stave with one hand and feeling the surface of the object with the other.

The chest? Bingo.

Which was good, because the confining darkness wasn't doing my anxiety any favors. I could already feel my pulse accelerating and my chest tightening. Shapes seemed to loom out of the silt. A figure grabbed for me. I shouted—big mistake, because water streamed into my big mouth—and slashed at it with the pulsar stave. The shadowy figure dissipated as the stave cut through, leaving bubbles streaming in its wake.

Then the chest bucked underneath.

My foot slipped. The one without toes, prosthetic from the knee down. Sure, it absorbed tachyon energies from the pulsar stave through me, but that didn't mean it had great tread. I'd have to have Liz rig up an improvement.

And the plate-sized mutated symmachite hurtled up at my face.

Yikes! I'd seen *Alien*, and *Aliens*, and—too many of those movies. I had a flash of a giant version of a tick, with bizarre designs on its legs and body that could have been designed by Dr. Victor Frankenstein himself. Hundreds of tiny golden barbs undulated on its underside. No mouth though, so probably wasn't going to implant eggs in my sternum.

I let myself sink to the muddy bottom of the pond. Sticks poked my ribcage. I let loose a blast from the pulsar stave. Bad idea. My aim was off because of the stupid churned up water, everything around me distorted and not where I thought it was. And the blast itself? The turbulence from it made the visibility worse.

The cyber-spider veered down, away from my face, which gave me an adrenaline shot of hope— until the creepy critter lassoed its tentacles around my fake leg. And pulled.

Pain lanced up into my muscles. I couldn't move. I was stuck. Trapped ...

Blackness pressed in on the sides of my sight.

One way out.

I twisted the stave-ax one last time. Its energies fizzled as my consciousness started to bleed away. Soon it'd be useless, because I'd be knocked out.

So, I cut ...

A sizzling reached my ears. The cyber-spider

flinched, unraveling its tentacles, and shot up through the hazy water.

What happened? The stave? It had repelled symmachites from my body—from everybody's body, I remembered. And the leg channeled energies from the pulsar stave … Must've had the same effect.

That's all I could put together when it came to rational thought. Fantasies of graphic death and suffocating pain overrode my head. I couldn't even swim.

Finally, my toes located the chest again.

It roared.

Like, a chorus of roars, dozens of them of varying pitches, warped by being in a box full of air underwater. It jolted me, and I pushed off, arrowing toward the dim outline of the island's submerged slope.

Had to reach it. Had to get out of the water.

Had to breathe.

I scrabbled through roots. Come on, Mercury. Get out of your own head. The cyber-spider … It was escaping. Up to the island.

Where Loredana waited.

I surged onto the miniature shoreline, panting, shuddering. Sounds became clearer as water drained from my ear.

Gunfire.

Not a crazy shootout—brief controlled bursts. Flares in the dark.

"Mercury!" Loredana yelled. "Mercury, I need

you to activate the stasis weapon! I cannot bring it online without the pulsar stave."

Crap. Because I was the only one who could make it happen.

Backpack. Sitting by the raft. I sprinted for it.

Loredana was in a crouch, firing at the creature, which wasn't easy because of its acrobatics. It bounced from tree to tree, emitting a constant, grating buzz, like a saw blade. Twice, it came within a tentacle's length of cutting her but Loredana dodged. She brought the pistol up and fired again. She missed.

Since when did Loredana miss anything?

I yanked the stasis gun free of the backpack, glowering. She really did want the thing intact. Fine. I jammed the pulsar stave home and lifted the weapon.

The beam sliced the night air, forming its signature cloud around the top of a tree. Bad news: the cyber-spider somersaulted off the top and landed beside Loredana. Who did not blast the thing into pieces.

"Move!" I shouted.

Loredana dove into a cluster of shrubs. "Go!"

I fired again. The beam went too wide, encasing another tree in a cloudy stasis field. A bunch of moths froze midair.

Another shot. Another miss. The cyber-spider turned toward me.

"Come on!" I snapped. Why couldn't I hit the thing? The weapon was vibrating so much ...

Wait a second. The weapon was fine. I was the one making it vibrate. Because I was still shaking.

The creature hurtled at me, again, just like underwater, and I fired.

The beam struck its right legs—finally, a hit!—but it kept on coming. It glanced off the gun and ricocheted off my shoulder. A searing cold cut through my chest and left arm, sending pins and needles through my skin, deep into the muscles. Felt as awful as the few times I'd been snagged by an astral fiend hungry for my body's energy.

Thankfully, this guy only got a nibble. It was enough to throw me onto the ground.

A thunderclap flat stripped branches off a tree overhead. I rolled over and stared up at a rip—or rather, the pint-sized equivalent of its nastier big brother. Think the top of Oscar the Grouch's garbage can.

The black hole wreathed in crackling purple lightning was a perfect fit for the obnoxious, buzzing cyber-spider, which vanished into it. The rip snapped shut with a second *bang*.

After the furious sounds of our brief fight, the continuing downpour was downright comforting. My head dropped back, right into a mud puddle. With a rock in the center. Because, yeah, a headache was a super fun addition to exhaustion running its course.

"Mercury?" Loredana knelt beside me. She looped an arm under my shoulders. "What happened?"

"I … don't know." Not true.

"Are you hurt?"

"Bumps and bruises. The usual." I grimaced as I

got to my kneels and then stood. "We'd better find out where that thing went off to."

"I shall contact Elizabeth." Loredana lifted her phone but didn't make a call yet. "Are you certain you're all right?"

"Pretty sure we both know the answer to that question." I removed the pulsar stave from the stasis initiator and wiped mud off its tail end before—well, great. My jacket was balled up on the ground, with my shirt tucked inside.

"There's no need for a tone." Loredana put her hands on her hips. "Had I known your plan—"

"Which went down the tubes once I got in the water. Yeah, I know."

"I'm not casting blame."

"Maybe I am, okay?" I ran a hand through my hair. "Give me a minute to process."

She turned away, her posture stiff as a pine trunk. I sighed. What, three months in and we get a nice argument in the middle of a mission?

"Look," I said. "I have to—"

"We have to go."

I shrugged. "As soon as Liz tells us where."

"No, Mercury." Loredana headed for the raft, Hub slipping in the mud behind her. Concern laced her voice. "We must go *now*."

That's when I saw the flashlight flickering like a nightclub's strobes.

CHAPTER SIX

By the time we rowed back to the shoreline behind the nearest houses, more lights joined the show. Red and blue ones.

Really hoped it wasn't Homeland Security. Because if they got here as fast as we did, I'd have to wonder if they had anything better to do with taxpayer dollars.

"Come on! You guys have to get out of here!" Oz was slinking around the base of the trees like this was *Platoon* and he was about to go all Charlie Sheen on the enemy approaching from the street.

"Relax, kids." The rain had let up to a drizzle, which gave me a chance to slip into my shirt and drag my jacket back on. Wasn't dry as I would have liked, but hey, I wasn't freezing anymore, so, bonus. "We've had a lot of experience talking our way out of these situations."

"Though I would rather avoid them." Loredana sounded weary. My body felt the same. She yanked another cord on the raft and it deflated so fast I wondered if there was now a giant gaping hole underneath. "Help me stow this, would you?"

We rolled the sopping wet bundle up into her backpack, which bulged against the hasty packing job. It was worse than repacking your luggage at the end of a vacation. I dismantled the oars and shoved them into my pack, alongside the stasis initiator.

"It's probably Mr. Hardt, from the gatehouse." Iggy frowned. "I can tell him you guys had to leave and … We set off firecrackers! That's why he thought he heard guns shooting."

"Good plan, kid. But let's check out who our visitors are, first, because if it's local PD, they might not fall for that. And Hardt already thinks we're here from the police."

"Duh, Iggy," Oz said.

"He didn't tell us that!" Iggy snapped. "Shut up!

"Truce, gentlemen." Loredana touched their shoulders. "Thank you for your assistance. If there are times in the future in which you may need our help, or you come across instances of the, how shall we say, strange, do not hesitate to contact us."

"Are you seriously gonna give these kids your business card?" I murmured.

"We can find your website and email her," Iggy said.

"What's a business card?" Oz asked.

Loredana smirked at me. "How does it feel to be among the newly aged?"

I shook my head as our group crept through the backyards, toward the street. Made it easier to see what kind of response we were dealing with.

Downside? It wasn't Hardt. A black sedan, unmarked except for a federal government license plate, was the source of the flashing lights.

Upside? It wasn't a random collection of agents. Bowe got out of the driver's side door. Three more agents—one Latino woman and two white guys who could have been fraternal twins—joined him.

Sorry, did I say upside? I meant, double downside. Or whatever the term is.

"Guys, do you have a shortcut home?" I whispered. "A way to get to your house without being spotted?"

"Yeah." Iggy pointed down the block. "But we have to go down by the Kuzara's and cross the street—"

"Mercury!" Bowe didn't need a bullhorn. His voice carried sharp enough he could have announced for high school football from the top of the bleachers unaided. "I know it's you. Come on out, you hear? We pulled your images from the gatehouse."

I rubbed my forehead. Mercury Hale, ace monster slayer, less-than-genius undercover investigator. "Cameras."

"Yes. I counted three." Loredana stood. "Come along."

"You're just gonna walk out there?"

"We can hardly afford to dodge Homeland

Security while we're attempting to retrace the cyber-spider," she said. "I will gladly accept one adversary instead of two."

"Bet he's got a different opinion." I shook my head but made sure I caught up to her before we left the cover of the bushes.

"Hey!" Oz blurted. "What about—?"

Iggy's hand clamped over his mouth. Oz glowered. His jaw twitched. "Ow!" Iggy hissed. "Don't worry. I'll get him—Ow! *Quit biting*. – I'll get us home, Mercury."

I didn't answer the kid. No point drawing Homeland's attention to them, as big of trouble as we were gonna be in.

"Mercury Hale, again." Bowe tipped back his blue ballcap. The yellow and white bobcat symbol shone in the streetlight. "And your blushing bride. Congrats, Mrs. Hale."

"Lark-Hale." Loredana stood toe to toe with him. The Homeland agents encircled us, with the twins reaching for their sidearms.

"My mistake." Bowe waved his guys down. "Easy, fellas. Jimenez, how's about you offer the happy couple a ride to the office in our vehicle? Vitarelli, you and Passarella take their rental. I bet Loredana here's got the keys."

"We're perfectly capable of traveling without escort," Loredana said. "What may I ask brings you to Whispering Pines?"

"It isn't the need for a nighttime stroll in the woods

of a gated community." Bowe jerked a thumb back down the road. "Residents heard gunshots. Security guard told them everything's fine—one big happy federal law enforcement task force, cooperating with local cops."

"Don't bother with the interrogation routine, Bowe." I tossed the pulsar stave end over end in my hand. "Syndax didn't show. Bummer for you."

"So, what, you all were taking target practice out by the pond? Lousy weather for it."

"Nicer looking than the kitten on your hat."

Bowe scowled. "Montana State Bobcats. Eleven-four last season."

"I'm sure the mommies and daddies paying tuition are proud."

"Don't go cracking on my alma mater because you didn't take my warning seriously."

"Gentlemen." Loredana raised an eyebrow. "Agent Bowe, unless you have orders to detain us, I suggest you stand aside so we may reclaim our vehicle. Your interference is inhibiting our ability to resolve a critical matter."

"Could be I do have those orders." Bowe propped his hand on his holster. I swear he managed to make his badge shine no matter where he was standing or how little light he was in. "I wouldn't recommend testing them. Don't think Homeland's forgotten how Serena vanished from your supposedly top-secret facility."

"I don't know what you're talking about.

Our office is under construction after the terrible earthquake it suffered."

"Right." He shook his head. "The earthquake and subsequent explosion, that had nothing to do with all of San Camillo Bay hanging in the air over the city, while a whole bunch of people shot at monsters and the undead."

"Good memory," I said. "Want a gold star?"

Bowe pointed a finger. "Just you—"

"Agent. Bowe." I didn't know about the stubborn guy standing across from her, but I wasn't about to contradict whatever Loredana had to say. "Stop your posturing, please. It's unseemly for man of your caliber. If you had been authorized to apprehend us, or even detain us for a short interval, Procyon's board would have been warned, and my manager Mr. Alvarez advised. Thus, I would have had foreknowledge. I do not. Therefore, I can only surmise your instructions are to surveil and report."

She walked around him, heading down the street like she expected me to join her for an evening stroll along San Camillo's Promenade. The Homeland agents swiveled, like they were gonna give chase, but then they glanced at Bowe, one at a time.

Bowe didn't give orders to arrest us. He didn't even bother placing a phone call. He lifted his cap, scowling, and repositioned it.

I grinned and trotted after Loredana. Had to clap him on the shoulder as I passed. "Keep that hat, Bowe. Rain might come back."

We holed up for the night at a Hyatt near Oklahoma City's airport. It was past midnight, which was becoming a pattern I didn't enjoy. Of course, I was kicked back in a chair by the window, watching the city lights on the horizon.

"I'd have thought you would be exhausted." Loredana approached from the bathroom, wearing a robe. She toweled off her hair, the red even bolder again the white fabric. "We had better rest."

"Had to check on Liz's scans. She sent them over. I hope she gets some sleep, too."

"The woman has caffeine for blood, I'm sure."

"Yeah." I tried a smile, but it evaporated, a lot like our chances of capturing the cyber-spider had.

Out the window, cars trickled down the streets. Not a wild town this late—or early.

"We really should get rest." Loredana's hand grazed the back of my neck.

"Keep that up and I won't get any rest." Smirk Attempt Number Two failed.

She flicked her fingers. I knew the gesture. As soon as I lifted the phone and sat up from my slouch, she alighted on my lap. "You're troubled."

That got a snort out of me. "I think everybody we know would agree."

"Don't be obtuse."

"My specialty." Ah, there went the grin.

Loredana's lips pressed firmly together. An

eyebrow lifted.

"Yeah, it was the same deal—the panic. I couldn't get a hold of myself. There wasn't any reason for it this time. No debris falling. No boardwalk crumbling. At least that made sense. But this was just water."

"Memories are powerful. Traumatic ones even more so." She turned my chin so we faced each other. "Perhaps we need to eliminate this memory with a more pleasant one."

"Like our honeymoon."

"Among others."

The kiss burned whatever lethargy fogged my senses. I ran my hands up her back, fingers pulling at the robe. But a doubt scratched at the back of my brain. Loredana's face, determined, focused, as she shot at the cyber-spider ... My lousy shots as I tried to capture it.

Failure.

Oh, no. Not now.

It should not surprise you. The catalog of your failures reaches beyond dimensions, Mercury ...

The voice was resonant, and chilling. It faded from a man's tones to singsong and feminine on the last word as it faded in my head.

The Whisperer, merged with Marigold Yen, plus bits of Alexander Arkwright snide arrogance. What a combo. They liked to mess with my mind, because through my vanquishing of them, they got linked to me. Doesn't seem fair. Vanquishing should afford a guy perks, right? Not punishment.

I'd been able to keep them at bay, and their murmurings to mere nuisance. But now the voice—or voices—rumbled through me as clearly as if I were listening on my earbuds.

Keep this up and you'll be known more for what you do wrong than what you do right. Poor warrior, poor leader, poor husband.

I broke from our embrace.

"What is it?" Loredana cheeks were flushed. Her eyes searched my face, as plainly as if she was seeking her next target. "What's wrong? Are you still hurt?"

"No. I'm good. I'm fine."

She touched my cheek again, but I intercepted her hand. "Sorry," I said. "I need a second."

"You can tell me what it is that bothers you, Mercury. We're not to keep secrets from each other, even in this line of work."

"I know. It's …" I blew out a breath. "Let's leave it alone, okay? I need to check in on Liz's results."

"That is what we should both do." Loredana pushed away. She found her phone in the pocket of her jacket, which hung next to mine on hotel-provided hangers. A dark splotch of damp carpet broadened as they dripped. "Since we have abandoned this topic."

"Come on, don't do that." As soon as the words left my mouth, I wished I could have blasted them midair before they got to my ears.

"Do what, precisely?" Loredana swiped into her phone without matching my gaze.

Keep your stupid mouth shut, Mercury Hale! But

I couldn't help it. The abrasive panic of the day before and this night had worn away my filter. Which sucked for everyone who wasn't me. "The thing where you wall off as soon as we disagree on something."

"It has nothing to do with disagreement, as you categorized it." Her voice was as cool as the frost on the edges of the windowpane. "I ask you a question and expect honesty in return."

"Look, some stuff isn't as easy to talk about, especially when it involves freaking out because of something that could have killed me."

"Then perhaps Doctor Becker was correct in his assessment. You should have been benched."

"Are you serious?" A distant part of me hollered that she was digging because I'd hurt her feelings. Another part argued that she made valid points and I was the one being the jerk. "How do you not get what I'm going through? When I pulled you out of Arkwright's temple on Meda, you were all set to walk away from Procyon and me!"

Ouch. Wrong thing to say. Big time. Loredana did meet my eyes, and I could tell I'd crossed a line. Aching from my own pain, I'd sought out and ripped the bandage off hers. Why'd I bring it up? We both knew how hard it had been, getting through those days after I'd rescued her—after she'd spend weeks in an isolated dungeon on a foreign world.

She was near tears.

"Elizabeth's analysis is nearly complete. We'll review her findings in the morning." Loredana snapped her phone down on the bedside table and hurried back to the bathroom.

"Hey, Loredana, wait ..."

The door slammed shut. Water ran.

Man. I wasn't one to agree with the Whisperer's haunting messages, but he wasn't far off. Botched the Syndax fight, lost the cyber-fiend, and got on non-speaking terms with my newlywed wife in less than forty-eight hours.

I got up from the chair and made it halfway to the bathroom door, intent on salvaging something from the mess, when the voice rolled over me like a wave. A wave filled with jagged debris.

Whatever you say will make it worse. She is proud and strong. You're not fit to heal the wound you inflicted, Mercury, when you cannot heal yourself.

"Shut *up*," I growled.

Don't blame us for revealing the truth, the voices hissed. *The truth being, you're as scared and vulnerable as the little boy left wailing in a pizza parlor by dead parents. Failures who begat a failure.*

A cold sensation erupted at the small of my shoulder blades.

I shouted and spun toward the wall, pulsar stave alive with blazing energy. Sparks erupted—but not from the weapon. I'd sliced a desk lamp in half.

Loredana emerged from the bathroom, in her "prickly" pajamas. She took one look at the ruined lamp and shook her head. "Good night."

"Hey, wait." I sat on the edge of the bed.

But she was already sliding under the covers. Her eyes were rimmed with red. She sniffed, as if she'd developed a sudden cold. Yeah, right. "Good night, Mercury."

"Loredana …"

"Good night." She rolled over. A hand tugged the comforter over her shoulder.

I gazed at my bare feet, hands gripping the edge of the bed. I let the pulsar stave roll onto the floor with a muffled clank. Dead metal, once it was out of my grasp. "Sorry. I love you."

Nothing.

So, I sat awake in the chair by the window, watching those lights again, wondering how many other guys fouled up so badly they were looking back in my direction.

Man. Really wished there was an astral fiend to slay right then.

Water.

I swirled around. Couldn't tell down from up, back from front.

A massive, shadowy bulk surged beneath—wait, so that was down. And there were ripples of white lights above, past the water's surface. Floodlamps?

Three rusted funnels yawned. Orange flames sparked from inside.

If it was under water, how was it on fire?

The arms shot up through the darkness, twisted

amalgams of flesh and metal, stabbing through my chest.

"Ahh!" I sat up so fast I fell sideways out of the chair.

"Well. Good morning." Loredana was dressed and ready to go, casual slacks and professional blouse. No trace of our blow-up. No indication she'd been upset—Except, of course, for the steely way in which she regarded my fallen state. "I trust your late night of study was productive."

"My late—Ah, oh." I fumbled for my phone. Sure. Liz's scans. "The cyber-spider's signature wound up in Florida. That's—weird. A long way off from San Camillo."

"Quite. I have made a few calls. There will be a car waiting for us when we arrive." Loredana grabbed her backpack. "Do be ready for departure."

I was pretty sure I was gonna still be laying on the floor in shorts and a T-shirt when she took off for Miami, so I got dressed faster than I'd ever slipped into the supersuit.

CHAPTER SEVEN

It was a short flight to Miami—a couple of hours. Short, at least according to my watch. I spent the time absorbing the data Liz sent along about the cyber-spider.

Which was better than trying for awkward conversation over what felt like a hundred years.

Loredana and I didn't speak for the entire trip, except for her checking into Air Traffic Control and me cracking the occasional joke. Spoiler alert: I didn't get any laughs.

In fact, we both did such a great job stewing that I nearly took off a thumb when I slammed the door shut on our rental Lexus.

"For heaven's sake, if you've something to say, out with it," Loredana snapped.

"Yeah? I figured silent treatment was our new thing." I made a show of checking my watch. "You know, three months into our marriage."

"Disputes happen, Mercury, even among spouses.

Ours may become more fraught by simple virtue of our complex occupation."

"Doesn't make it any more fun." I glanced at her as I steered us out of the parking lot. The car swerved sharply into the road, earning me a long, irate honk from a moving van that I'd cut off. Served me right for driving angry. "Okay, look, I get that I shouldn't have locked myself up like I did. It was wrong. We should be talking this stuff through. Together."

"That is the promise we made. Together, always."

"Right." Heat rose to my face as I remembered some of the stuff—as in, epicly stupid stuff—I'd said the night before. "And that was way out of line for me to bring up your stay at Hotel Enemy Fortress."

Loredana smiled, a small curl of her lips but I'd take it. "No, not your wisest move. For my part, I had no intention of interrogating you. And yes, perhaps I should not have 'walled off,' as you so delicately stated. I wasn't acting in my role as handler or head of Operations—I was worried for you. Because I love you."

"That's what made it so hard for me to …" I drummed my hands on the steering wheel, like the beat could make the words form faster and make them coherent. "I won't let you down. Not again. Not like when you were ripped right from my hands into the Interstice. So, when I panicked again, for no good reason, that failure latched back on. I can beat this."

She put her hand on my leg. "Post-Traumatic

Stress is no simple ailment like a headache or an upset stomach."

"Believe me, I wish it was, because I could pop a Tums and get rid of it."

"Doctor Becker could have prescribed medication—"

"No." I grimaced. "I mean, it's not a bad idea. I just don't want to rely on a pill to keep me stable."

"There's nothing shameful about managing an illness such as yours. It's easy to think of it as a failing, when in fact what you're dealing with is as real and worthy of treatment as any other."

"I get that." Movement in the rear-view mirror drew my attention as we rolled out onto the Dolphin Expressway. White SUV. Nothing odd about that, unless you count that its twin was in the next lane over, two cars behind it. "This is me, though—the superhero. I can't rely on something like that when I'm the one who's got to go out and fight monsters. No way side effects can come into play."

"Reasonable. But I don't want to see you harm yourself out of a misguided sense of masculinity."

I snorted. "Don't worry. I kill interdimensional murder-beasts for a living. Not really worried about society's view of how manly I am."

Loredana chuckled. My heart jumped—there was the sound that kept me happy. But it occurred to me, that was the point. I had to take care of me, sure. Being run down physically and mentally meant I'd be no good to anyone. Her happiness, though, had to be paramount to mine.

Ramos had taught me that. Well, lectured me.

And I'd seen it firsthand with his family.

"Well, sorry, again, for being a jerk," I said.

Loredana leaned across and kissed my cheek. "Apology accepted—wholeheartedly, this time."

"You mean you weren't sincere last night?" I fanned myself like I was gonna faint. "Heavens."

She play-punched me below the ribs. "Twit."

I laughed, then switched lanes without signaling. No honks—seriously, people using their blinkers were in the distinct minority on this road. I checked the mirror.

White SUV Number One changed lanes to match. Its twin changed lanes the opposite direction, then began a slow acceleration.

"They're not terribly subtle." Loredana reached into the passenger seat for her bag. "Considering the dearth of other cars."

"You noticed our caravan buddies?"

She raised an eyebrow, frozen in mid-motion, with that expression she put on that reminded me of an elementary teacher disappointed in a dim student.

"Right." We were a few miles away from the I-95 exit. "We want southbound, right?"

"Yes. To Miami Beach." Loredana removed an MP5 and drew a magazine from a side pocket. She could have been consulting her phone for the weather.

"Glad you didn't try to take that through TSA," I murmured.

"Having one's own plane does have its advantages. Operationally speaking." She prodded my shirt—this time, under the right arm, where the pulsar stave hung in a custom harness designed for concealment. "I daresay there'd be more questions in your case."

"Touché." The SUVs changed lanes again, adjusting their travel around the pattern in the cars near us. It left the first SUV one sedan behind us and its buddy approaching on the left, up a clear lane.

Two of its passenger side windows rolled down.

"Hang on." I peeked right. No cars, just the side of the road. Good.

I slammed on the gas and swerved into the left lane, accelerating ahead of the second truck.

Gunfire blasted through the empty space where we'd been. The first SUV barreled into the lane behind the second, causing a flurry of honks. Glad they didn't cause a wreck. Not that those guys seemed worried about keeping a low profile.

I changed lanes as fast as I could, one eye on the speedometer as we hurtled through traffic. It was spread out, which was great, until we rounded a curve and hit what I term—technically speaking—as a traffic turd. You know what I mean. A handful of cars bumper to bumper, plodding along, as if the speed limit out on the expressway wasn't fifty-five.

"Braking." Loredana rolled down her window. Hot, sticky air roared in.

The SUVs raced up behind us. More gunshots cracked.

Our back windshield and the left rear window shattered, reduced to a crumpled spiderwebbing of holes and cracks.

"Shooting!" I yelled.

Loredana gestured to our left. I swerved into the next lane, the Lexus at a 45-degree angle to everyone else, then cut back to the right—which gave her a nice field of fire.

No messing around, then. Loredana fired a continuous stream of bullets at the first vehicle. In a few seconds she'd emptied the magazine, and the first SUV had lost its driver's side windows. Gained a jagged pattern of holes along the door, too.

"Not bulletproof!" I shouted over the gunfire and wind and general cacophony of car noises, including our own engine, which growled like an angry bear. "Bonus!"

"Exit approaching!" Loredana let the magazine drop to the floor and slammed in a new one.

I found a gap in the cars ahead and steered through. Thought we'd lose the rearview mirror on my side. The driver whose BMW I almost sideswiped must have thought so, because his passenger, an elderly woman with more fake tan than the president of the United States, stared at us as I zipped by. Southbound exit onto I-95 was a quarter mile ahead.

Bullet zinged off the Lexus' roof. I veered over two lanes then back one.

"Kindly hold steady!" Loredana was backwards, shooting in short bursts at the second SUV. The first one had fallen behind, parked by the side of the expressway. Men in T-shirts and a combo of jeans and khakis helped an injured person out of the driver's seat.

Exit lane. I put my blinker on and made for the lane, right before those fun white slashes painted on the concrete roadway.

The second SUV's engine roared over the rest of the traffic noise as it bore down on us. That guardrail was getting way too close.

"Left!" I yelled.

I swerved in the aforementioned direction, slinging us back into the main travel lane, coming a foot from the bumper of a looming semi. His horn sounded like the anger of God Himself, if, you know, he was prone to shouting.

Didn't stop there. We careened across the lanes and zipped up the exit ramp northbound, the Lexus bouncing along the pavement and—well, crap, that was the concrete barrier.

I jerked the steering wheel but not soon enough to avoid ripping the rearview mirror on my side clean off the car. Pretty sure I left a stretch of gashes along the doors, too. By the time I'd stopped swerving and the car quit behaving like a jackrabbit on a sugar high, Loredana was hunkered down in her seat.

"This is explains so many of the reports I've seen you file with regards to automotive damage over the years!" Loredana said.

"Hey! In my defense, most of those were monster-inflicted, and in at least three of them, *I wasn't even driving*!"

"Mind the road, will you?" She reloaded again, muttering, "A long gun would have been more useful to pack for such a situation ..."

We barreled down the ramp and back onto six lanes worth of vehicles heading north up the Florida coast. You couldn't have asked for a more gorgeous day—the sky was turquoise and cloud-free. Palm trees shuffled under the influence of a breeze. Even the graffiti festooning commercial flattops off to the right was a rainbow of bold, clean colors, and who doesn't like a good festooning, am I right?

Downside was, not only had the SUV kept up with us—albeit separated by a couple cars—but a white Nissan Rogue zipped up in the third lane. I'd given it maybe three seconds' thought of, "Hey, is that another bad guy ride?" when armed men and women fired on us from open windows.

"Cover!" I shoved Loredana's head toward her knees and ducked, too, as bullets punched through the glass all around us. What I really wanted to do was crank the steering wheel and plow those jokers into the median wall—because I was *not* getting run off the road by a soccer mom's ride. But there was more traffic out here, even though drivers seemed smart enough to back off from our crazy chase caravan.

Of course, there was another way to handle this. Up close and personal. My favorite.

"Take the wheel." The gunfire slackened,

presumably so the hit squads could reload and communicate as to whose turn it was to shoot something. I unbuckled and dropped my seat back.

Loredana grabbed onto the steering wheel and contorted herself until her legs were squeezed by mine. Her shoes scrambled for the pedals. I backed out, shimming over the reclined seat into the back. The Lexus swerved and slowed, but only for a moment. Loredana slid the rest of the way into the seat, taking my place, and the seat slammed up against her back. "I would ask what you had in mind, but I will doubtless disapprove."

"Better to beg forgiveness than have to ask a committee for permission." I plucked the pulsar stave from its holster under my shirt and powered it up. The blazing yellow-white light surged across the runes, crackling between my fingertips. One more thing. I rummaged in my pocket for a black mask that would cover the lower half of my face. Hey, if it worked for Dominic when he was incognito, why not me?

Besides, I didn't have time to change into my supersuit.

"One can hardly call me a committee, Mercury."

I leaned over and kissed her on the cheek. "Close enough, Your Highness."

She sighed. "*Star Wars*?"

"You know it. Stay close."

I channeled energies into the pulsar stave and blasted the passenger door free.

There was this split second of nothing, like I'd paused a video game—the Rogue full of the hit squad with bullets frozen en route, the door horizontal to the blurred highway, Loredana's hair twisted in front of her face. Nothing like a moment to examine the situation, courtesy of the stave's power leaching into my body.

Now would be the time to not screw this up. Don't know if that counted as a prayer; don't know if I even needed one. But hanging around Ramos a lot had taught me to not discount the possibility that the Big Man was listening. Ramos sure hung his hat on the fact.

I flung myself across an empty lane, bounced off the ruined car door, and time sped back up.

My timing was awesome. Managed to land square atop the SUV—and much to my delight, the dummies who'd either leased or rented this rolling gas-guzzler had opted for the fancy model. You know, the one that came with a moonroof.

A burly black man and two white women—one blonde, one brunette, stared up at me in that split second before I bashed the glass in with the stave.

I dropped into their midst, which I figured was a great idea, because then they wouldn't try to shoot me, right? Well, they must have also decided that was a possibility, because extendable batons struck out at me the instant my feet hit the seat cushion.

There I was, standing half out of the broken moonroof, wind whipping my upper body, while my legs got the beatdown. I needed more room to fight.

So, I cranked as much energy as I could from the stave and spun it in a blistering circle right above their heads. Metal and plastic sizzled where the energy blade scythed through the roof supports. Glass melted.

And the roof flipped off the Rogue like a kite with cut strings.

The only vehicle impacted by my less-than-safe move was the SUV, which had snuck up on the Rogue's rear—and got the huge hunk of metal as an extra hood. The SUV's tires squealed, it jackknifed, and flipped into the median. Last I saw of it was the bent wreckage of a truck.

Fair enough.

The four people in the Rogue had wisely ducked my roof-slicing action. I bashed the blonde woman in the head, knocking her senseless. The black guy swung his baton, but I met it stave-first, reducing it to bubbling plastics. He screamed as the sizzling mix burned his hands.

And his eyes widened, giving me a great view of how purple-tinged they were.

Syndax. Great.

"Nice look," I said, before flipping him into the remnants of the trunk space. Huh. Surprisingly roomy.

The brunette in the front passenger seat managed to get her gun back, a big semi-automatic pistol of a model I didn't have time to determine, because she shot at me point-blank. News flash: I couldn't deflect bullets like a Jedi with a lightsaber. I mean, I probably could have, given substantial prep time. But the best I could do was flip up and over onto the hood.

Kudos to the driver for keeping his rig on the road, by the way. He was a lanky redhead whose eyes were black as tar from his tachyon infused Syndax dose.

"Pull over!" I gestured at his roof. "You lost your deposit anyway!"

He drew a pistol, but I was already moving, onto the bumper. Yes, the front bumper. No, it wasn't a good idea, but I really did need him to stop.

Because at some point in my ill-advised rampage, he'd swung behind the Lexus and was accelerating to ram it.

We'd already passed an exit. And there were either concrete barriers or metal guardrails making it difficult to get this vehicle slammed against one side of the road or the other without ejecting me. Because, clearly, no seatbelt.

So, I stabbed the pulsar stave into the pavement.

It flashed so brightly I thought I was gonna need LASIK surgery after the fight was done. Chunks of freeway flew up and over. The Rogue started to slow, but the driver pumped the gas in response. The engine thundered in my ear, which was mere inches from the grille.

Good news? We were drifting into the righthand lane, thanks to me using the stave as a makeshift boat tiller.

Bad news? My arms were giving way.

The brunette lifted her gun—and I don't know where she'd stashed the rifle, but she'd apparently decided an M4 automatic would be more effective. She shot across the hood, missing me.

But blowing out the rear tires of the Lexus.

It swerved from side to side. I had no idea how Loredana could handle it in a pursuit like this. But I was praying, whether you think it was a stupid idea or not.

Because the road bridged a canal a few seconds ahead of us.

The Lexus made it across, scraping its passenger side along the rails of the breakdown lane. Which meant Loredana had either been hurt or survived well enough to steer.

Either way, I wasn't gonna let these two take her out. I swung the stave up and over, ready to impale the engine—

When an old red pickup with jacked-up wheels rammed the back of the Rogue.

We fishtailed, skidding toward the bridge and the canal just over its edge, right at a gap between barriers meant to prevent what we wouldn't avoid—taking a swim.

Wasn't about to stick around.

I leapt up over the last two conscious Syndax goons, hurtled across the pickup's roof, and bounced into the truck bed. My prosthetic leg gave way on impact because, naturally, I hadn't braced myself well enough in the hurry.

The Rogue barreled on the wrong side of the railing and nosedived into the canal with a tremendous, steaming splash.

I gasped, trying to catch my breath as I lay on my back and watched greenery whip by at the fringe of my vision. The truck slowed. Its horn honked in the most obnoxious, redneck way. I was expecting "Dixie."

"Mercury!" Twin backpacks dropped onto me. Loredana's face, blood streaked down her temple to her jawline, appeared like a vision of an angelic being. "Stay there!"

"Y'all hush and buckle." A slow, smooth male voice answered her. "We've got a rendezvous to keep."

Don't move? Accept the free ride?

"Whatever you say, Cletus," I muttered, and closed my eyes.

<h1 style="text-align:right">CHAPTER
EIGHT</h1>

Guess what? His name wasn't Cletus. It was Randy.

Our rescuer—hang on, assistant rescuer, because I had the situation totally in hand—took us on a winding right up and down what felt like every side street in North Beach, Miami. Not to be confused with North Beach, San Camillo, which wasn't nearly as pretty and still bore scars from repeated astral fiend attacks.

Loredana embraced me as soon as I staggered out of the pickup's bed. Wish I could have rested up for a bit. My otherworldly origins meant I could heal faster and absorb more damage, but man, getting smacked around still hurts.

"Y'gon need medical attention?" Our rescuer leaned against the open door of his pickup truck. Calling him square-jawed was to put all squares everywhere to shame. Guy was rocking a sleeveless black T-shirt and rumpled blue jeans, and a mullet that would have done Kurt Russell proud. In fact, his entire look screamed *Big Trouble in Little China*. Eyes as bright as the clear sky were the only thing that made me think he might be dangerous—well, that and his muscled arms decorated with cross tattoos, one cluster on each shoulder. Were those drops of blood inked down his wrists?

"I'm good. Thanks. For that, and the help."

He pointed, without breaking his stare. "Might tell that to your leg."

I glanced down. Ah. The prosthetic's ankle was twisted 45 degrees. I braced it against the tire and shoved until it was in roughly forward orientation.

Loredana cupped my face in her hands, fingers brushing the whiskers which had miraculously sprouted since I'd foregone shaving a few days in a row. "Are you certain you don't need to be examined?"

"Only in the brain." I tapped the side of my head.

"Of that I have no doubt." She goosed me before presenting her hand to this Randy guy for a handshake so formal it could have been offered to a prime minister. "Loredana Lark, Operations."

"Randy Kyle." The drawl struck me as familiar.

Loredana must have been waiting for more, like specific title, because we stood there with seagulls for background noise. She arched an eyebrow.

"'Fraid that's all you're going to get, ma'am." Randy extricated a toothpick from his pocket and went after the gap between a couple teeth like he was heading up an archaeological expedition. "Cordelia don't prefer I talk to strangers about my line of work."

"We didn't figure you for a volunteer, Randy." I jerked a thumb at the parking lot and its motley collection of cars. We were a few hundred yards from the beach, surrounded by restaurants. "But if this is your secret lair, you've gotta up your game."

"You must be him."

"Well, since I'm not the *her* ..."

"Gentlemen," Loredana said. "Let's not keep Delia waiting, shall we?"

Randy made a gentlemanly bow and gestured for Loredana to cross the street. There was a Cuban restaurant called El Huerto on the other side, with a red neon sign that read "Closed."

I was a step behind her when Randy put a hand on my chest. "No can do, partner. Cordelia's instructions—Ms. Lark first, then us."

"How about you quit touching me and we try that again." I shrugged off his grip.

"Hold on." Randy lifted the edge of his shirt. The butt of a pistol protruded from behind his belt. "Just 'cause I heard stories of you don't mean I'm inclined to let you run all over creation without proper escort. 'Specially since Ms. Lark's been a guest before, and you ain't."

Ain't? Curiosity overcame my desire to remove this guy's head. "Come on. You're Operations, right?"

He shook his head. "Independent contractor.

Emphasis on 'independent.' But Cordelia and me, well, let's say we're old classmates. Share an alma mater and everything."

"I'll let you two compare class rings once I get inside. You've got to have some Procyon access, though, if you know who I am."

"Sure. It's informal." Randy grinned. "My old man was partial to a tall tale or two when he'd had enough whisky in his system."

Old man ... The mullet ... The drawl I now recognized ... "Jack Jackson."

Randy winked and pantomimed shooting me. "Circle gets the square."

"As in, *Hollywood Squares*?" I blinked. "Original or reboot?"

"Reboot. I ain't that old." Randy glanced at his watch—a smartwatch, I realized, with a black screen and the word "Proceed" glowing in gold. I'd have been less surprised if it were LCD and with a Velcro strap.

He led me over the crosswalk to the restaurant's white stucco front with long, narrow windows of tinted glass. A second sign underneath "Closed" read, "Take-Out Only" in English and Spanish, with a phone number available. Red and green Christmas lights framed their interior. The orange roof tiles were chipped, their flakes littering the sidewalk, but as Randy pushed open the door, I could have cared less. The beguiling aroma of ham and swiss Cubanos, the tang of ceviche, and the desire for a cold bottle of beer no matter what the brand left me salivating. I surreptitiously wiped the corner of my mouth.

Music drifted across the tables, a Latin beat that got my fingers tapping against my leg. What I wouldn't give for another dance with Loredana. We'd been out once a week since the honeymoon—nightclubs, dance halls, even a senior center. Hey, it was a fund-raiser for their new building and Loredana's a big deal in community relations.

Randy wove between the empty tables and leaned on a counter that was drowning in menus and tourist brochures. If you wanted to parasail, snorkel, or eat Stromboli while parasailing in a snorkel, the counter of El Huerto was the place to find it.

"Senor Kyle." The man behind the Square payment tablet—no old-school register, unless it was underneath—plucked a green notepad from the pocket of his floral shirt. He had curly white hair and a thick, wavy moustache. "What will it be?"

"Bottle of Corona for me, Eduardo. House Cubano, with pickles, for my friend." Randy produced a credit card from his wallet.

"Hey, man, come on. I'll get it." Provided I remembered my wallet, or card, or cash.

"Nah. Company money."

"Yours or Procyon's?"

Randy winked.

The owner ran the card. He shouted orders to the kitchen. Male and female voices shouted in response. "I will send when they're ready."

"Beer me first. Gotta check the pantry."

Eduardo retrieved a bottle from the cooler behind him. "You just add these to your stash, right? Never actually drink one?"

"I'm prepared. Like a Boy Scout." Randy slapped me on the back. "C'mon. Pantry."

Didn't really want to follow him but since I was pretty sure Loredana wasn't hiding in the ladies' room, I followed Randy to an alcove. A red curtain covered the back wall. He slipped between the folds.

Huh. Really was a pantry, stocked with every kind of canned bean and vegetable you could imagine. "This where they keep the salad fixings?"

Randy popped the top of his bottle and sipped it, as he counted down from the center of the top row, then over three to the right. He pushed the can of black olives.

The entire wall slipped soundlessly back three feet.

"Stay close. Arms tight." He shoved me forward.

"Listen." I stood close enough to get a whiff of whatever product he used on his locks. The floor wasn't tile there. My shoes scraped metal. "If you keep with the hands—"

We dropped so fast I swore I'd left my stomach ten feet above.

Blackness shut off the square of light overhead. My eyes strained in the dim yellow bulbs set into the walls and the floor. The corridor stretching ahead of us was barely wide enough for me to extend my arms. Puddles littered the concrete. The rumble of machinery drowned out most other noises. I spotted the glow of electronics in a brightly lit room about twenty feet ahead.

"Don't want to leave the ladies waiting too long," Randy said as we headed for the light. "You know how they gossip."

I rolled my eyes. "That's literally what you're doing."

He chuckled, and I did my best to remain cynical and sarcastic—because inwardly, I was jumping up and down. Secret entrance! Underground base! Beneath a restaurant!

If Procyon's headquarters was underneath Carlito's and I had to smell pepperoni pizza all day, I'd never have any money.

We passed five metal doors, unmarked, stained with rust. Even the concrete walls felt damp. But the corridor opened into a room that shared a lot with Tracking back at home, only on a smaller scale—three desks with computer screens, scattered equipment lockers, and a big, sprawling monitor that took up a wall. Probably thirty feet long, and my height. It was just as damp in the room as it was in the hall. I wondered who thought it was a good idea to have a basement in this part of Miami—or any part, for that matter.

"About time the boys joined us." CCordelia Keyes leaned against one of the desks, with a tablet nestled in the crook of her arm. She was a tall, slim woman with high cheekbones and coppery brown skin. Her classy black skirt and jacket with a scarlet blouse were in direct contrast to Randy's casual Friday garb. "Good to see you, Mercury."

"Hey, Cordelia." I dragged a wheeled chair across the floor and positioned myself next to Loredana, who was working on a plate of nachos slathered in cheese and pork. "Good thing I got my order taken upstairs."

"We wouldn't want you to starve," Loredana said. "Delia and I were catching up."

"Saved the briefing for the grownups?" Randy propped his feet on a keyboard.

"Only so we don't have to repeat it, and with smaller words." Cordelia shoved his boots off with her tablet.

"Hate to break up the party, but when my food comes, I'll have to take your super-cool secret elevator back upstairs." I jerked my thumb toward the corridor.

An orange light pulsed next to a storage locker off to the left. Randy pushed his chair, rolling to intercept. He opened the locker and ... My sandwich?

I bet my jaw dropped far enough to create a second basement. "Your secret base has a dumbwaiter to the restaurant?"

"Got to stay subtle and fed." Randy handed me the plate.

I took a ravenous bite of the sandwich. "You guysh are th' besht."

Loredana snickered. "I think we can proceed, Delia."

"All right, kids. As you might have already guessed, Syndax is in town." Cordelia swiped a display on her tablet. "They've been staying low to the ground—until your loud arrival."

"Hey, the only thing loud was the automatic weapons fire *they* introduced." I used the sandwich to wipe sauce from my plate. Too bad I was on the clock. I could have used a nap after scarfing an entire Cubano.

"We did do our fair share in retaliation." Loredana crossed her arms. "Have you been able to deduce their aims in Miami, Delia?"

"*Si*. They're not subtle." Cordelia smiled. "If anything, they're clumsy. I suppose the repeated tachyon dosing doesn't improve their mental capacity."

Randy snorted. He swigged a bottle of Corona. "Dumber than a discounted box of rocks at Wal-Mart."

I didn't figure how that made the rocks dumber but, hey, his quip, not mine. "Let me guess: You've had them abducting and trying to sacrifice families so they could bring astral fiends over to Earth for late night snacks.

"That's a big negative," Randy said. "I've been tailing them. No abductions. Shoot, not even any gunfights until y'all showed up."

"They've focused their activities on charters."

Cordelia highlighted a section of docks on Miami's shoreline, tracing a loop on her tablet as the image repeated on the room's massive screen. "Deep sea."

"Charters. As in, boats?" I frowned. "Don't tell me they've taken up fishing."

"I doubt it. More likely, they're looking for something." Cordelia brought another screen up, this one filled with numbers and calculations and all kinds of formulas I had trouble with in high school. Still had trouble, actually. The only math I wanted to do was when it came to my paycheck and how much got eaten up by the feds and the State of California.

"I trust Elizabeth was able to forward the scans she has undertaken in pursuit of our quarry." Loredana snitched the last pickle from my plate before I realized her hand had moved. Man.

"She did, and her data helped us correlate the strange readings we've been getting off the coast. Procyon's satellites and oceanic buoys kept pinging fluctuations in background radiation—nothing bad, but nothing good, *tampoco*."

The map expanded, taking in the Caribbean and eastern Atlantic. I grinned as I recognized the contours of the region. Any connoisseur of the weird—and popular culture—would recognize the area beyond the Bahamas, with Puerto Rico and a certain tiny island to the north. "They're going to the Bermuda Triangle."

"I'll be," Randy murmured.

"Syndax isn't the only one." Cordelia swiped one

more time. Two red dotted lines crept out across the USA and wound up in the leftmost corner, near the edge of the Bahamas island chain. "These are the routes Liz calculated. Spatial distortions preceded by tachyon bursts. One began in Oklahoma City before ending here early this morning."

"The cyber-spiders." Loredana pursed her lips.

Randy chuckled.

"Good name, right?" I nudged Loredana. "See, he agrees."

Loredana shook her head but continued, "Delia, can you give us precise coordinates to this rendezvous? I would very much like to be on site so we can apprehend both creatures."

"We can get the wheels in motion, honey, but it's not a simple matter of walking down to the quay and hailing a boat like you'd call for a taxi."

"Yep." Randy snapped his toothpick and tossed the pieces into a trash can. "'Specially with all the ruckus you pair caused. Cops are going to keep a close watch on the roads ... Hold the phone. Your car."

"Is trashed, yeah, good memory." I rolled my eyes.

"No, genius, I meant, it's no trick to pull the plates and see where it came from. As in, the rental agency. As in, the airport." Randy frowned. "Surprised I ain't seen your faces splashed across my phone."

"Procyon will deflect any fallout from the unfortunate incident on the freeway," Loredana said.

"No doubt Delia is already aware of the necessary machinations."

Cordelia smiled. "You're not wrong. I'd give up Whoopie pies if I never had to have another phone call from Hector Alvarez."

I winced. "He knows?"

"How can the man not? Law enforcement calls the airport—and that gets TSA involved …"

"Homeland Security, too." I rubbed my forehead. Suddenly I was glad Loredana had stolen the last pickle, because my appetite vanished.

Randy tapped my shoulder with something cold and solid—an unopened bottle of Corona.

"Thanks." I pried the cap off with one end of the pulsar stave and took a decent glug.

"Unreal," Cordelia murmured. "Did he just use the weapon—?"

"I've found it best to not dwell on the idiosyncrasies of his personality." Loredana gestured to the map. "Back to our procurement question, if I may."

"Of course." Delia was still frowning at me. "Like I said, I can get you a boat, but it'll take some doing. Give me twenty-four hours. That'll also give you time to recover from your ordeal and for some of the heat to die down."

"Wait for Miami to come up with more crime." Randy belched and wiped the back of his mouth. "Make you old news."

"Solid plan." I clinked my bottle with his. "So,

who'd you have in mind for a boat captain on our—how long of a cruise is it, anyway?"

"About six hours to the coordinates," Randy said.

"Teacher's pet," I muttered.

"I'm the pilot, bonehead," he said. "For your boat."

"Oh. Right." I drummed my hands on my thighs and stood up. Oof. Too fast. My stomach churned Good thing we weren't going anywhere soon. "You guys got a place to crash?"

"The hotel. Randy will take you down the passage." Cordelia stared me like I was an exotic creature—probably zoo-level exotic, not as weird as a cyber-spider. "I'll text you the particulars this evening. If Syndax makes a move, be prepared to accelerate the timetable. But our best bet is to depart tomorrow morning. This may not be as simple as it seems."

"Is it ever?" Loredana and Cordelia hugged. "I look forward to hearing from you."

Randy slapped my back. Again. Next time, no joke—I'd whack him with the pulsar stave. "Catch you later, Dee. Come on, Mercury. Let's go find what's behind Door Number Two."

I made a show of crossing my index and middle fingers on both hands. "If it's anything other than a hidden passage to a nearby hotel, I'll be bummed."

Randy did the finger-guns thing and led us back into the dark hallway.

CHAPTER NINE

Water.

I swirled around. Couldn't tell down from up, back from front.

A massive, shadowy bulk surged beneath—wait, so that was down. And there were ripples of white lights above, past the water's surface. Floodlamps?

Three rusted funnels yawned. Orange flames sparked from inside.

If it was under water, how was it on fire?

The bulk hurtled toward me, pushing the water aside in a torrent of bubbles.

Shipwrecks don't rise!

I swam for the surface, but even with the energies of the pulsar stave lingering in my body, I was too slow. Everything was too slow.

The arms shot up through the darkness, twisted amalgams of flesh and metal, stabbing through my chest.

"Mercury?"

Rain tapped on the floor-to-ceiling window of our hotel. Dawn turned the sea and sky pale blue beyond the ghostly beach.

I rubbed my face. The bed made me feel like I was resting on a cloud—as if I'd ever taken a nap at a couple thousand feet up. Wonder if Airfoil had ever tried it.

Loredana was at the door, her reflection in the wall mirror to her left frowning with equal concern. She had on a dark windbreaker and pants, like she was going out for a walk, except I was pretty sure she had at least three weapons concealed on her body.

"Hey." I sat up and forced a grin. "Rough night's sleep."

"Indeed. Cordelia is downstairs. I shall check in with her, but I expect we'll move out in a bit. Gather your things."

"Staved up and ready to go." I tapped the weapon. It sat on the other side of the bed.

"Meet me in ten minutes." She blew me a kiss and closed the door.

I blew a breath and sagged against the pillow. Rain hissed again. This wasn't gonna work. How was I gonna stay in the best shape if I couldn't get through a simple shuteye without having the same freaky dream over and over again? At least I had some more details to go on, this time.

"When will you know more?"

"When it's ready to reveal itself."

That was what Edie had said to me. A hint from her would have been nice. Instead, I was stuck with debilitating panic. There was no denying it, even if I didn't remember the dreams—the shortness of breath, the sweats. I was sick of the attacks. I wanted to be the one attacking.

But I wasn't ready. Just—scared.

I growled and pushed off the bed. Screw that. I had to be ready. If it meant faking it, fine. Other people were relying on me. Procyon. Loredana.

Took me a couple minutes to slip on a black jacket and lace up a pair of boots. I tucked the pulsar stave into its harness, then grabbed my phone.

I needed to talk to someone. But Loredana was in Operations mode. Not that she didn't understand. The fear, though …

It wouldn't let go.

I dialed.

The voice on the other end answered in four rings. "Mercury? It's 5 am out here. I'd heard you went on a vacation. Second honeymoon?"

"Ramos, I'm freaked out and I don't know what to do."

Ramos didn't say anything for such a long time I thought he'd hung up. When he did come back, the wry, stern tone was gone. "Okay. Explain it to me. From the top. I assume this has to do with the Promenade."

"How'd you—?"

"Wilhelmina. She's worried about you."

I shook my head and mouthed bad words away from the phone. "She shouldn't have butted in like that."

"Well, if you survive your mission, be sure to chastise her when you get back." Ramos snorted. "I'll bring popcorn for that argument."

"Focus, man. I'm serious."

"I know you are. What are you afraid of?"

"She probably told you."

"Doesn't matter. I need to hear it from you."

I paced the hotel room, tapping the phone on my lips, heart hammering. Why couldn't I admit it? He already knew I was afraid.

"The water?"

"Yeah. Getting back out there. *Under* there. I thought it was just the pier, like underneath the Promenade, but the same thing happened at a stupid pond in the middle of Oklahoma. What am I supposed to do when we get out on the open ocean? Because that's where we're headed."

"Fear's strong, Mercury. Stronger than we think is possible."

"Tell me about it."

"I am, if you'd keep your trap shut. Don't you think I've been afraid?"

"You never act like it."

"Every time we've faced monsters, I've been scared out of my wits. I don't want to die. If I do, I know where I'll end up, so that's not the issue—I have faith in the promises I've received. But dying? That's not something I relish the thought of."

I leaned my forehead against the window. "I don't know if I can do this."

"You can. And you will. Because no one else can. This is your path. Do you think you'd be able to stand against evil without God on your side?"

"I'm not a church boy, Ramos. Pretty sure he's got your back more than mine."

"He'll still use those who don't believe. And when it comes to fear, he's the one who takes it all away. That's why I stay by your side when the terrors come charging at us from dark dimensions." Ramos' voice shook, but I didn't the feeling he was afraid or upset. There was a passion to his speech that I'd heard— well, from no one else. "I stand because I have to push back the fear for myself and focus on others. If I don't fight, what happens to my city? What happens to my family? That includes you, son."

Ah, he did it again. I blinked rapidly.

"The best I can do is pray for you. I know people mock that all the time—thoughts and prayers versus actions. There are enough warnings about faith without deeds to keep me convinced. But there's power behind that, too. Not the same as the power of the pulsar stave or the power to open a rip between dimensions, but powerful all the same."

I pictured Ramos in his cell on Meda, locked there for months by Arkwright, clutching the crucifix in his hands. I saw him puncture the impenetrable barrier around Arkwright's portal in Cavill Cemetery, finding a way to our enemies when nothing I did made a scratch. Maybe he was on to something. Maybe I could shift focus. To others, instead of me.

Hey, look. I don't want to be afraid. I know I've screwed up—a lot, across a bunch of years. But I have people depending on me. I have a job to do. It'd be great if you could help. Ramos has something I lack. Think about it, okay?

It was silly and trite. My face burned with embarrassment before the last sentence formed. What was I gonna do, though? I was desperate.

"Deliver us from evil," Ramos murmured. "Forgive us our sins. Fallen, but not forgotten."

I wiped my eyes. "Thanks, Ramos."

"He's there with love for you, too, Mercury. Give him time. His will is one we don't often understand—in fact, we can't."

"Think his will prevents major malfunctions on my part?"

"I know you're stuck in your head. But you can't go alone on this one. Trust me."

My hand sprawled on the window. Left a print in the condensation. He was right. When was he not? I was waiting for the day Ramos' advice proved bogus, but I'd be better off watching for the sun to fail rising.

"Ready?" He asked.

"Sure." Or not. I blew out a breath. "Enjoy your morning. I've got a boat to catch and personal demons to slay."

Our quartet wound up at the piers off Alton Road, across the channel from the local Coast Guard base. Cordelia and Randy did all the talking to the scrawny Asian guy in baggy shorts and Marlins ballcap. I waited with Loredana in Cordelia's BMW, watching the negotiation through the shimmering raindrops caught in the car's headlights. Sure, it was past 8, but it might as well have been evening with the gloom.

Twenty minutes later, Randy piloted us out of the channel on our very own speedboat.

Okay, so it was more luxury sedan than race car—Baia Atlantica 78, sleek and white, its hull reflecting Miami's lights as we slipped from the channel. But she was fast enough. Randy opened the throttle up to 50 knots as we emerged into deep waters, sending us slicing across choppy waters.

Six hours' ride on a dark ocean wasn't as fun as it sounded. I took advantage of the gorgeous, wood-trimmed main cabin to go through one-man sparring drills with the pulsar stave. The wobbly deck underneath helped a bunch, actually, forcing me to concentrate not on just my aim but my balance. Easy to imagine an astral fiend's tentacles slashing at my arms and legs. Or a cyber-spider's sharp, knobby arm tearing through my skin.

The nightmare boiled at the edges of my memory.

Let it out.

Shut up, Whisperer.

Embrace the fear. It can drive you to defeat your enemies. Fear makes you desperate. Desperation gives you an edge when you fight without restraint.

I snarled and swung the pulsar stave through a brass-coated railing. Searing energies left a sizzling gash four inches across, an ugly scar.

Great. Here was hoping Procyon's budget for this foray covered incidentals like rage-induced damage to a quarter million-dollar yacht.

The engines slowed. Had it been six hours already? I checked my watch. Five and a half. Close enough.

I went topside. The rain had intensified. It was a good thing the Atlantica was a hardtop. I zipped my jacket collar. "Are we there yet?"

"How did I know you were going to ask that?" Cordelia was scanning the sea with a pair of night vision binoculars. Good thing, too. There was no way to make heads or tails out of the horizon, not in the gloom, though when I stared long enough, I could make out the difference between the murky, undulating waves and the solid steel horizon.

Hold up. There were lights flickering.

"Another vessel." Loredana had a pair of binoculars, too. "Range?"

"Mile and a half."

"Ain't gone sneak up," Randy said. He nursed the engines, the Atlantica creeping through the troughs and over the crests. "We get any closer, they'll light us up—with bullets plus actual lights."

"You're not wrong," Cordelia murmured. "Mercury, here."

I took her binoculars. Yeah, sure was another ship—a fishing trawler, bigger than the Atlantica. Five people on deck. More silhouettes in the lit cabins below. Some carried long rifles. "Definitely Syndax. And it's a safe bet they're out here for the same reason we are."

"I'll take that money," Randy said. "But if they are, they're dumb."

"You mean because they juice with dangerous particles derived from another dimension? Because I'd agree."

"Nah. Their boat. She's all wrong." Randy flicked his fingers, his palm resting lazily on the Atlantica's wheel. "Fishing smack. It don't even have its cranes deployed. They might could net tuna but they're not hauling anything off the floor. Not when it's a hundred feet."

"That's it?"

Loredana nudged me. "We're holding position over a shallow portion of the seabed, not far from Nassau. Average depth within a three-mile radius is two hundred fifty feet."

If her word wasn't good enough—which it was, duh—I had the depth finder as proof. That light-colored blob surrounded our boat and spread far enough to encompass the Syndax craft. Okay. So, they didn't have a crane that could go deep enough. I peered through the binocs again. No sign of diving gear, either. The people on deck were watching the surface.

And a couple were watching the sky.

My nightmare flashed before me, but this time, it wasn't accompanied by a spike of terror. One portion—the funnels underwater, the strange glow, the hulk rising in a rush of bubbles.

"They're raising a wreck," I said. "They're gonna bring it to the surface."

Randy frowned. "Welp, sure, there's a couple of wrecks down there, but sound like you missed the part where I said they all got an itty-bitty crane and any one of those wrecks are too big to haul."

"Not how I would have put it, but Randy's right." Cordelia pivoted, checking the area around us. "No sign of any other ships incoming, either. If they've got something that can salvage—"

I shook my head and pointed up. "They're watching the sky."

Loredana reclaimed the binoculars. Her fingers tightened. "My word. He's right."

I chuckled. "Don't sound so surprised."

"Well." She smirked. "Miracles do happen."

"Don't make any sense," Randy muttered. "What're they bringing, one of them big old Russian choppers? Even they're not powerful enough. That wreck's got three funnels. Has to be four hundred feet long. Old freighter or liner."

"Perhaps they only need a portion of it," Loredana said.

"That still doesn't tell us how they plan to sever part of the wreck and bring it up." Cordelia glanced at me. "Assuming we can verify your intel."

"Coming from a recurring nightmare? Your call. I'm trusting the source." I tapped the side of my head.

"When did these dreams begin?"

"After my conversation with Edie." I nodded at Loredana. "While you were waiting outside Forecasting."

"*Alabao*!" Cordelia looked at me like I'd sprouted tentacles. "Edie? Forecasting? You actually hired Edith Pathkiller on as your Forecaster?"

I nodded. "She's, ah, pretty accurate. And somewhat scary."

Cordelia socked Loredana's arm with a playful punch. "And you left that out of our chat. I *knew* I'd heard correctly. There you were, playing it for rumor."

Loredana smiled. "One has to keep certain aspects of the job close to one's chest, in these uncertain times. It's a matter of security—hers and ours."

"Oh, I understand." Cordelia adopted a fake pout. "Just you wait until you need vital intelligence and I play coy."

"Uh, ladies?" Randy gazed through the window canopy. "Think the chopper's here."

The clouds warped. Rain falling at an angle bent horizontal, spraying like a sprinkler head. A dazzling white light shone down, targeting the fishing boat. One of the men on deck waved both arms.

The light shifted away from the boat, onto the ocean.

"Sneak us up, Randy," Cordelia said. "While they're preoccupied."

"Nice and stealthy." All out lights had long been doused, so the Atlantic stayed a dim wraith as Randy brought us around in a loop. Our course wound us down toward the fishing boat.

The chop got worse, until Randy killed the engine. "Rough stuff. It's coming from just off their bow."

That was because the water was swirling.

Whirlpool.

"They're—remaining stationary." Loredana spoke like she didn't believe her own eyes, or the words accompanying them."

The whirlpool grew, throwing up a spray as thick as rain in reverse. Randy restarted the engines, just to keep us from being drawn toward the maelstrom, which was a good thing, because something was emerging from the center …

The rusted top of a funnel.

Then, in short order, a second, followed a third.

We all stared. Nobody had anything clever to say.

When the miniature storm subsided, a ship sat on the surface. It was a looming hulk of a freighter—not a lot of portholes in the rusty hull, but plenty of rips and tears. The bow and stern were gone. It looked like they'd been ripped free. An orange glow seeped through the seams.

"Okay," Randy finally said. "Guess they didn't need the crane."

My line, pal.

Loredana touched my shoulder. "Nor did they need a helicopter."

Sure wasn't a vehicle descending. Because the small, dark shape behind a blazing spotlight settled on the fishing boats was nowhere near the size of a chopper.

It was a person in a gray cloak and a faceless mask.

Cordelia made the sign of the cross. Twice.

Randy growled and reached for a rifle with a scope.

"That's not Airfoil," I said. "And I take it the Garrison gang he's affiliated with doesn't dress in creepy fashion."

"Certainly not," Loredana murmured. "This is the Ashen."

Supervillains?

Great.

CHAPTER TEN

It was bad enough we couldn't get any closer to the formerly sunken ship without drawing attention from who knew how many Syndax mercenaries aboard the fishing trawler. We were lucky the Ashen person hadn't spotted us.

Because if he—or she, I guess—did, we'd get ourselves crushed in a gravity forcefield.

Yeah. The Garrison and the Ashen were two sides of a secret society coin, entities opposing each other in their concealment of powerful medallions that let the owner manipulate localized gravity. Brandon Tusk had one of those. He broke the rules and established himself as the superhero Airfoil before helping me save San Camillo from destruction.

He did the latter by holding up a giant lake in the sky, preventing it from drowning my city. So, made sense I was nervous about the bad guy who had the same powers.

"How bad is it?" Cordelia asked Loredana.

"Syndax forces in San Camillo were using the cyber-spiders in their attempt to breach the Interstice, with moderate success. Leaving them in their hands doesn't bode well for us. Or for anyone, for that matter."

"But you still want to take it intact."

Loredana glanced at me. "Even if we sink the ship, they shall raise it again."

"Not if we scatter the pieces," Randy muttered.

"Look, I can blast the sucker with the pulsar stave, but it's not gonna do a bunch of damage against a boat that big." I looked at everyone in turn. "Which means, you're talking about something that can produce a bigger bang."

"C-4," Randy said.

"No, Randy." Cordelia shook her head.

"I'm sayin'! We got enough on board—"

"Explosives were not discussed as part of our infiltration option." Loredana crossed her arms. "Not to my recollection, Delia."

"They were a backup option. Not necessary, but helpful. You know me." Cordelia smiled. "I like my options."

"Hey." I rapped the pulsar stave on the wheel. "How's about we figure out how we're all gonna board that ship without being noticed? And tossed through the air like a toy a kid in the bathtub got bored with?"

Bad news: The answer was swimming.

Or scootering, I mean.

We slipped into wetsuits and donned compact SCUBA gear, with enough air for us to get over to the risen wreck plus the return trip and some extra. I tested the air and made sure the mask fit. Could have used the supersuit, for amped up power, but the thing wasn't waterproof, and I didn't want to freeze to death on my way to battle.

"Randy, make sure the boat's ready." Cordelia stuffed an Uzi into a dry bag. She, like the rest of us, also had a combat knife lashed to her thigh.

Randy saluted. "You bet." He disappeared onto the bow.

"Hate to break it to you, but I'm not a fast swimmer." I was keeping an eye on the fishing trawler, which bobbed against the shipwreck's hull. A bunch of guys attached lines, bringing the two vessels together.

"Not a problem." Cordelia pulled a tarp off a row of what looked like black bullets with twin fans—sea scooters. "Just be careful where you park."

"And where precisely did you have in mind?"

"The stern. Or the gash where it used to be prior to the wreck being broken up. Around the other side from our nosy guests."

Randy rejoined us. He and Cordelia got into the water first. The hum of the sea scooters was almost lost under the hiss of the rain and the rumble of the waves.

Loredana caught my arm. "Are you with me?"

"In both ways." I kissed her. "Don't worry."

"Stay by my side and we'll make it."

No time to freak out now. I secured the pulsar stave and made sure my own dry bag—the one containing the stasis initiator—was hooked to my belt. Then I splashed into the ocean.

So far, so good. My body held together even as my mind searched for new and fun ways in which to panic. I kept replaying my conversation with Ramos, focusing on his words, his voice, and then pulling in pieces of our old conversations. You know, the ones in which he was arguing with and/or yelling at me. Good times.

It was a necessary distraction from the depths. We were maybe twenty feet below the surface, with little illumination except from glow sticks attached to the undersides of the sea scooters. Speaking of which, "scoot" they did—eight miles an hour felt quick when we had to cross about a mile's worth of open sea.

Having other people around finished the job my replay of Ramos' chiding had begun. My brain went mission-only, to the point I found myself wishing I had my playlist blasting from my earbud. Oh, well. No sense in ruining a good thing.

Our formation stayed tight, but staggered, so no one was blowing bubble trails from the sea scooters' fans in anyone's faces. The wreck's hull was easy to spot, because the orange glow stayed as constant as a campfire's coals. Cordelia and Randy steered right, dipping down toward the jagged edges of the ship's missing stern end.

Loredana and I followed our local guides into the gaping metal wound. We surfaced in a long, open compartment with bowed ceiling and bulging walls. Every surface glistened with decades' worth of sludge and slime overlapping chunky rust.

Cordelia stowed her scooter to one side. Randy had already abandoned his ride. He knelt by an open hatch, a TEC-9 aimed at the dark opening.

Both had suppressors for their guns. Loredana drew an HK45 semi-automatic pistol from her dry bag and affixed a bulky silencer of her own.

I joined everyone at the hatch, with the pulsar stave powered up and split in two. "Who gets to go first?"

"Guy with the magic sticks," Randy said. "'Less you wanna rock paper scissors for it."

"I though you were gonna say ladies first."

"Seriously?" Cordelia brushed between us. "Follow my lead and try not to kill anyone on our side."

I hopped through the hatch before Randy could recover from our mutual chagrin. Loredana followed, holding up her cell phone. The tachyon dowser on the underside pulsed as we made our way forward. Randy watched our backsides—at least, I hoped not literally, because that would be Loredana's backside and nothing about that was okay.

Not that I had anything to worry about. Randy was the one who should be worried. Because if Loredana caught him, well, he'd have more fun if I beat him up with the pulsar staves, let's put it that way.

We'd just checked the first intersection of corridors when the entire wreck shook, like someone had backhanded it. I braced against a bulkhead which, thankfully, didn't crumple under my arm. I wondered for a second when my last tetanus shot was.

The throaty roar of an explosion cancelled that segue.

Randy checked his watch and grinned. "Not too shabby."

"Good timing, on your part," Cordelia murmured.

"Never been late yet. Good thing, too, since it's C4."

"Since when did you have time to plant explosives on the fishing trawler?" I asked. "Not that I'm complaining."

"Ain't their boat."

Loredana covered her mouth at the same time I slapped my forehead. "You blew up *our ride?*" I hissed. "What're we supposed to do, swim back to Miami?"

"We take the Syndax vessel," Cordelia said. "Destroying the Atlantica provided a distraction."

Sure enough, I could hear distant motors starting.

"Inflatables." Loredana nodded. "You're splitting their forces."

"Misdirect, Lori. Classic."

"Yes, quite, though again, communication would have been welcome."

Cordelia shrugged. "Sorry. Not used to sharing."

"Tell me about it," Randy grumbled. "Y'all want to have a town hall debate on this or we gonna find our creepy critter?"

"Critter." I nudged Loredana. "You've got the dowser. Better if you lead the way."

"My thoughts precisely."

We rearranged our positions so I could walk a step behind Loredana, with Cordelia right behind me.

"Still can't believe you'd spend all that money on a boat and then blow it into a million pieces," I whispered to her.

"Not our boat. Not even Procyon's."

My momentary relief vanished under a tidal wave of worry. "It's—not a government boat, is it? Like Homeland, or FBI?"

Cordelia shook her head. "Heroin dealer. He owed me money after I did him a favor."

"What favor?"

"Rescued his granddaughter from Syndax. She's fine. But then I found out he tried to sell Randy and me to Syndax instead of being appropriately grateful."

"So, you stole his yacht and blew it up."

Cordelia's smile seemed a lot less friendly in the light of the green glowsticks. "Sometimes when you gamble, you lose."

Note to self: Don't play poker with Loredana's best friend.

The wreck must have been a cargo vessel,

because we traced the tachyon emissions through a maze of passageways and across yawning storage compartments, none of which were fitted out like cruise liner staterooms. Sludge was heaped in corners. Fish flopped in pools left behind from the ship's resurrection. No human bodies, though. Which meant we only had to deal with the dark and the cold and the sensation that we were being watched.

Orange light seeped through cracks as we got closer to the signal. I could have sworn the pulsar stave was vibrating, but maybe it was a phantom thing, like a phone you think is alerting you but it's not.

"You know," I whispered to Loredana. "We forgot something."

She raised an eyebrow. Worth whole sentences.

"Hub. The robot container."

"Yes. I realize that. Hardly a simple matter to bring him out to sea. He's stowed in the airplane."

I made a circle motion with my finger, as if I could encompass the entire situation and the spooky old boat. "So ..."

"We shall simply have to improvise."

To be fair, she was wearing the gloves Liz had designed. Yellow and black patterned hands clashed so badly with the sleek wetsuit I felt like I should quip about a fashion faux pas. As grim as everyone was, and as quiet as they kept, I figured it would be in bad taste.

See? That's maturity.

Metal slammed against metal forty feet ahead.

I ignited the pulsar stave. A muted gunshot barked. Something whizzed by my head.

"Stand down!" Cordelia hissed.

I glanced back. Randy had the TEC-9 raised to the ceiling. A tendril of smoke curled from the muzzle. "Seriously? You could have taken my ear off!"

"Nah." He resumed his crouch. "Only if I was aimin' for it."

"Not comforting."

"What was it?" Cordelia asked.

"Part of the bulkhead collapsed," Loredana said. "Unsurprising, given the dilapidated state of the craft."

Shouts erupted in the distance. We all brought our weapons up and, thankfully, Randy didn't try again to blow my head off.

But someone else was shooting. The *crack* of automatic gunfire was clear enough, if muted by distance through who knew how many rusty metal walls.

The screeching noise? That was new.

Orange lights rippled to the right—I mean, starboard side. Should've brushed up on my nautical lingo before we hopped off the Atlantica.

Cordelia motioned with her right hand. Randy pressed against the bulkhead, hidden in shadows. Loredana backtracked down a set of steps and propped her arms at the top, for a stable firing platform.

"Guess the guy with the glowing weapons stays out in front," I said.

Cordelia smiled and pointed up.

Ah. Lots of places a guy could wedge himself up there, between pipes and steel supports. I jumped at the bulkhead, pushed off at an angle, and swung into a prone position. Took some grunting and twisting to get myself turned over so I was facing down, and when I did, Cordelia had vanished. Too many dark hiding spots to figure out into which one she'd scurried. Heck, the only reason I could see Randy was because A.) I knew here he'd gone and B.) he snorted and spat onto the deck. Classy.

I saw Loredana sighting down her weapon. She winked at me

Footsteps. "Hey! There's a guy on the ceiling!"

Guess I should have paid closer attention instead of winking back.

I swung down, feet slamming into the back of the Syndax's mercenary's head. There were two muffled gunshots and the second guy's kneecaps went red. The pulsar stave clobbered him in the face mid-scream.

Two down and out.

"Shoot." Randy worked a toothpick like a pry bar. "Guess y'all don't need me. Want I should go for a swim?"

A yelp. I whipped around, but instead of a third Syndax soldier ready to kill us, there was a limp form sprawled on the deck beyond the next hatch. Cordelia stepped over him, wiping the blade of her combat knife along her sleeve. "Keep moving. They'll be spreading out around the ship."

"Chasing the same quarry, no doubt." Loredana indicated the tachyon dowser. The red lights told us we should head farther to port. Problem: No hatches in that direction, or bends in the hall.

Solution? Pulsar stave.

I cut a blistering outline through the bulkhead, metal sizzling and spitting. The rough oval sloughed off, splashing into the next compartment. Loredana clambered through first, with a small flashlight affixed beneath the barrel of her pistol.

The ship shuddered again. Metal squealed, like we had collided with something else, but it didn't feel like we were moving.

"Another bomb?" I asked Randy as he climbed into the compartment.

"Not ours, if it is."

"Mercury." Loredana waved the phone-slash-dowser. "Continue."

"I love it when you get all terse and commanding." I started cutting through the next wall.

"Yes, well, were I to become monosyllabic, perhaps that would teach you to curb your verbosity."

Randy chuckled as he chewed on his toothpick.

"That means you talk too much," Cordelia whispered to my right.

I rolled my eyes. "Never heard that one before."

The cut was complete, but the section was stuck. I went a little crooked and the piece didn't flop out like the last one. Sue me. I hauled off and kicked it.

A three-foot-wide piece of metal fragmented underfoot, and my leg punched through the remainder like I'd stepped into wet cardboard.

And one of the cyber-spiders flung itself at my face.

I dropped onto my back, in part because like I already said, I'd watched all those *Alien* movies and didn't want any of those nasty, ragged pincers near my chiseled good looks, and also because I figured the thing's sudden appearance would prompt my three teammates to empty entire magazines of bullets at it.

Right on both counts.

The cyber-spider might as well have been a figment of our imagination, because every shot either missed it or sparked off its hide—which, it should be noted, had taken on a cracked appearance, like the surface of a dry lakebed. Difference was, instead of darkness in those cracks, orange light fizzled out. Also, it had grown. We were now dealing with a mutated critter the size of a German Shepherd.

"Why do they have to grow?" I snarled and flipped back onto my feet.

"Don't destroy it!" Loredana hollered.

"Yeah, I know, on it!" I yanked the stasis initiator from my belt.

"Down!" Randy tackled Cordelia, who shouted. Sounded like she was annoyed she hadn't been able to line up another shot.

Just as well. I didn't need a frozen Procyon

Intelligence person to drag back through the bowels of this damp old dump.

The stasis beam struck the cyber-spider as it sprang off the opposite bulkhead for a second attack. The creature twisted mid-air, shrieking like a cat whose tail got pulled, only a thousand times more hideous. The mouth—scratch that, *three* mouths—on the belly was an addition I didn't recall from Liz's tutorial.

But it hovered in that cloud of distorted light, stuck.

I shouldered the stasis initiator and sighed.

"No time for rest, sadly." Loredana brushed strands of wet hair from her face. "One cannot expect our interlude to have gone unheard."

"Like the frickin' Fourth of July," Randy muttered.

"Hey, nobody made you go all Rambo, even with silencers," I snapped.

"Suppressors." Cordelia was checking the hole through which the cyber-spider had emerged. Another corridor?

"Whatever. Loredana?"

"I have it." She had her sleeves rolled up, exposing the custom gloves Liz had loaned her. Purple sparks skittered around the cyber-spider's cocoon of light as she touched it.

Metal groaned. Why did it keep doing that? I looked up.

Wrong, as our president liked to say. The noise

came from below. The deck shuddered.

"Rats," Randy grumbled.

The floor collapsed like a soggy paper towel. Next thing I knew, we were in freefall.

And the splashdown was a cold shock two seconds later.

CHAPTER ELEVEN

I thrashed around for a hand, a step, a railing, anything I could use to drag myself up out of the water. No dice.

The water was frigid and murky, a soup of nothing. Where were the bulkheads?

My feet touched bottom. Finally! I crouched and then pushed off, catapulting to the surface.

I gasped, water streaming from my face and stinging my eyes. Who knew what gunk I'd have to wash off? Sure, it was good-old fashioned salt water from the Atlantic, but how much of it had been sloshing around inside the wreck, picking up chemicals and such?

Loredana surfaced beside me. She treaded water, arms otherwise occupied. She'd managed keep the immobilized cyber-spider in her embrace. "Mercury!"

"Hey! You okay?" I paddled over. The pulsar stave glowed, lending much-needed light to our surroundings.

"Yes. No injuries. The stasis field appears stable."

"Good." I grinned.

"What is it?"

"You kinda look like an otter floating on its back with an urchin for lunch."

She smirked. The submerged kick to my ribcage wasn't unexpected.

Cordelia popped up, followed by Randy. He shook his head like he was a dog who just disobeyed his master's command to *not* jump in the lake, and then slapped the water. "Bracing!"

"Not the swim I wanted to take." Cordelia wiped her mouth with the back of her hand. "Ugh. To think, I was reading on the beach in my bathing suit last week."

"Me, too." Randy swam to the edge of the room, where the deck slanted, and the twisted remnants of a stairwell clung.

"Don't remind me." Cordelia accepted his hand as he helped pull her up. "I was blinded by the white."

Randy winked and chuckled.

I nudged Loredana. "See what we miss out on when we hide in the bunker?"

"Focus, please, darling." Loredana pointed up. Lights streamed through the hole I'd broken in the wall on the deck above. Voices drifted down to us. "I think our enemies have ascertained our former position."

"Crap. Okay, let's hustle, gang!" I helped her navigate to the stairs. Randy and Cordelia guided her onto surer footing by keeping their hands on her shoulders. The gloves let off tiny sparks where she held onto the cyber-spider. Thankfully the gross critter didn't so much as flinch. Stasis for the win.

"Down there!"

Flashlights pinpointed us. I squinted into three blazing spots, wondering which ones were handheld and which ones were attached to guns. I mean, only for a second.

I whipped up the pulsar stave and let loose a blast of golden-white energies.

It burst dead-center to the Peeping Toms above, eliciting a chorus of shouts, some swearing, and a cloud of steam. Glass—the lenses of flashlights, I hoped—shattered and at least one bad guy dropped a gun, or so I guessed by the clattering on metal.

"Move out!" Randy shoved Cordelia through the hatch.

She didn't let herself get pushed too far, though, before she swung her right arm up and unleashed a volley from her Uzi at the same gap I'd targeted. Between the rattle and the shouting, I had no idea if she'd hit somebody, but we weren't sticking around to find out.

"Phone!" Loredana's snapped command jolted me as we pounded down the next corridor.

"The who-what now?" I glanced over my shoulder. No one chasing. But the Syndax mercs were running all over the place. Above us? In an adjacent compartment? I was no good figuring out where people were based on their footsteps.

Suddenly, Randy spun sideways. He let off a burst from the TEC-9, punching holes through the flimsy bulkhead. Someone cried out. A body thumped against the wall.

I stared at him.

"What?" He tapped his ears. "Hearing like a bat."

"My phone! Take it!" Loredana snapped.

Right. The tachyon dowser. She slowed her stride for a moment, so I could pull the device from her belt. It had gotten dunked like the rest of us, but I wasn't worried about the possibility of malfunction. No way she would have brought equipment so sensitive when we were on an underwater mission.

Plus, she still had her hands full.

I tried to decipher the blinking lights on the screen, listening for beeps among our clanking footfalls. "Keep going straight! Take the next left!"

Cordelia and Randy outpaced us by six feet. He skidded through the corridor intersection, gun aimed high and to the left. She crouched behind him, pointing right. Both muzzles flashed. Muffled reports echoed down the hall. A body thumped onto the deck, and a mangled cry preceded a second impact.

They had already taken the left branch as Loredana and I rounded the corner. Two Syndax goons down. No body armor—wetsuits, ammo belts, and H&K MP7 submachine guns. Their chests were soaked dark.

"We should invite your Miami buddies to more Procyon parties," I murmured.

"Directions, please."

Yep, she'd gone all taciturn. Which was fine. Couldn't have both of us slinging quips—that was my thing. "Hey. Hey! Up ahead! Next right!"

"Stairs!" Cordelia's comment cracked the air as soon as they disappeared in the direction I'd instructed.

"Ah." The indicator gave me numbers. "Up!"

They pounded up the flight, as Loredana and I joined them.

Randy reached the top first. "Hostiles!"

His TEC-9 opened up, rattling in the narrow confines. I slammed Loredana against the wall, gave her a kiss, and flung myself through a gap between Randy and Cordelia.

I'd always wanted to try outrunning bullets.

It was a close race, I gotta admit. I shoulder-checked the first Syndax guy, his expression hidden behind goggles and a mask. The blow flipped him onto his back, feet flailing toward the ceiling. Meanwhile, his buddy took the bullets from Randy's fusillade.

Two more behind them.

I separated the pulsar stave and slashed through a gun, leaving behind a molten lump and a screaming mercenary. Never got tired of that—the weapon melting, I mean, not the screaming.

The other one, Number Three out of Four, he was

a head taller than his pals and quicker. Forget the gun. A survival knife jabbed toward my ribcage. A second before it sliced through the wetsuit I remembered, *Well, crap, this outfit isn't damage resistant like the supersuit!*

Fiery pain lanced along my abdomen. I spun out of his reach, hoping no more bullets were coming my way, and parried a second stab with the pulsar stave. Another strike flipped the knife from his hand.

Then I put enough of the stave's energy toward my prosthetic leg, so the kick that came next sent him crashing through a crumpled bulkhead.

"Shoot." Randy joined me, his jaw working. Was he hurt, or—Wait. Where'd he get gum to chew? "Remind me not to rile you up."

"Don't piss me off and you won't be next." I reached into the compartment with my leg and prodded the guy. Out cold. "We're clear for now."

"Then keep us moving," Cordelia said.

Like I hadn't thought of that. We had one cyber-spider. The second wasn't far off. Judging by the readouts on the tachyon dowser, it was in the forward part of the wreck's broken hull, not far from where the bow had been ripped off when the Ashen raised it off the sea floor.

I led us through the labyrinth of corridors, up claustrophobic stairs, trying to keep the memories of near drowning from overwhelming my senses. The recent dunking hadn't triggered a panic attack, but it hadn't helped my sense of well-being, either.

I just wanted to sack out on the couch with Loredana, turn on some *Dr. Who*—or maybe *Star Wars*, if she nodded off—and down a couple slices of pizza.

But that wasn't gonna get the job done. And no matter how skilled these Procyon Miami folks were, they hadn't faced the things I had. They weren't the ones grappling with nightmares turned real.

The signal for the second cyber-spider grew more intense, the beeps building until they merged into a continuous tone, like somebody was leaning on the keyboard of a synthesizer. Very Eighties. A breeze cut across my face. Smelled sharply of sea spray. Not the stale stench of the wreck's interior, but the scents like I'd experienced on the Atlantica yacht during our crossing.

"Hatch up ahead," Randy said. "What're the odds they got the upper deck hemmed in?"

"Probably could, because we're not getting chased." I blew out a breath. "I can draw their fire if I charge in, but I'd rather not if someone's got a better idea because, you know—bullets."

Cordelia plucked a tiny gray object from a pouch on her belt—waterproof, I assumed. She unfolded black plastic strips and set it on the deck. Then she activated her phone, using the screen sideways like she was watching a video or, a better comparison, playing a game. Completed with a cross-shaped controller in the display.

"A drone?" I asked.

The miniature robot hopped off the deck and buzzed up the last set of stairs, disappearing over the lip of the hatch. I could still hear its rotors over the rainstorm intensifying, as sheets of water pelted the ship.

"Personal reconnaissance system. Gift from our armed forces." Cordelia smiled. "A senator owed me a favor."

"Delia has a way with such debts," Loredana said. "Thought the manner in which she collects them isn't always in line with Procyon policies."

I pointed at the frozen cyber-spider she clutched. "Says the lady holding a baby monster."

Cordelia shushed me. She chewed on the corner of her lip as the images on her screen whipped back and forth. "Coast is clear."

Randy craned his neck. "Yeah, no shadows where the bad guys could hide. Yup, none at all."

"Then if the drone's missed something, we'd better not."

Right. I clambered up the steps.

Rain slammed into me like I'd stepped into the path of a hose. It drove at an angle, hissing where it hit the superstructure. Waves churned around the broken hull, splashing up the sides, sea spray mingling with the downpour. I wiped my face twice in thirty seconds before giving up. At least if the Syndax goons showed up, they'd need windshield wipers for their goggles.

The deck was tilted, not bad enough I thought

I'd slide off, but I definitely wouldn't want to set the pulsar staves down or they'd roll into the ocean.

The fishing trawler bobbed a way off, with only a handful of people aboard. An inflatable dinghy was still out circling the debris left over from the Atlantica yacht. Still couldn't believe Randy had blown our ride sky high.

And the second cyber-spider came skittering around a funnel.

"Everybody stay back!" I backed off into a fighting stance, wishing for the second time I had those tunes. Forget it. I jammed one of the stave halves into the stasis initiator and let it power up.

The cyber-spider reared up on four of its legs and squealed. Ugh. Sounded like someone had married a pig to a crow, then poked their kid with a branding iron. Not a happy beast.

"Be careful!" Loredana emerged from the hatch.

"Hey, you're the one who has to juggle *two* of these when I catch it!" I leveled the initiator and squeezed the trigger.

The beam lanced out—

And splashed off the lopsided bottom of a funnel.

The cyber-spider was floating off the deck, rising into the rain. It writhed, claws grasping in vain to stop its ascent. The squeals got even uglier.

"Nobody told me the nasty creeps can fly." Randy aimed his weapon.

And the TEC-9 took flight, too.

So did Cordelia's gun, and Loredana's, and the

captive cyber-spider. The stasis initiator even yanked itself from my grip—but I managed to jerk the pulsar stave's half free and tuck it away.

"Lori, if you've got any ideas, let me hear them." Cordelia looked like she was ready to get into a brawl, too, arms drawn up to strike.

I shook my head. "No time. We've got to get off the ship."

Which I tried to do, but my legs wouldn't respond. Arms either. Worst part was, it wasn't an unfamiliar sensation.

Airfoil, aka Brandon Tusk, had held me in the exact same grip more than once.

Not ashamed to say, my heart rate spiked and the terror that had stayed bundled in the back of my brain unfurled. I would have rather taken another deep, dark swim.

The Ashen descended from the sky.

He floated onto the deck, gloved palms extended up, fingers curled. Gray jacket, gray pants, gray mask. I don't know whether it was the insane power he displayed by holding the four of us immobile, our weapons drifting in a circle six feet over our heads, or the cyber-spider suspended twenty feet over *his* head that impressed me the most.

"Dang," Randy muttered.

"I want to thank you for all the hard work you've done on my behalf." His voice was young, stern, with maybe a slight East Coast twang. Couldn't place it from behind the featureless mask. "Syndax's tracking devices might be good, but not as precise as yours. My compliments to your technician."

"Now would be a good time to surrender," I said. "And since I'm a nice guy, I'll let you call off your goon squad first."

"Thanks but no thanks. You've got a lot of myths circulating about you, Mercury. All of them fantastic—how you slayed monsters, dismantled Syndax, and saved your city from a being more powerful than anything the Ashen have encountered. And now you've tracked down a priceless prize. But I can take them to their rightful places."

Syndax soldiers swarmed up the companionway behind us and from around the funnels. Nine of them. I sneered. "Looking a little short in the manpower department."

"Mercury, do be quiet," Loredana murmured.

"He doesn't bother me, lady. I know his type. Like Airfoil." The Ashen shook his head. "Or so I've heard. Never had the pleasure of meeting him. But that'll change. We'll put these creatures to good use. After all, there has to be a way to harness the tachyon-based energies to our advantage."

It struck me then—maybe he didn't know. He hadn't seen my fight with Airfoil. And all the Syndax mercs who saw Airfoil go rogue at Mount Shasta were either dead or locked up.

The pulsar staves trembled as their energies sought an outlet. Easy, fellas. "Too bad for you you'll never get the secrets I already unlocked about those critters.

Oh, well. Better put bullets in our heads and smash us flat."

"What are you doing?" Cordelia hissed. "Are you insane?"

"Steady on." Loredana's tone brooked no argument. "Mercury is right, you know. I daresay there isn't a man alive who doesn't know more about the untold powers those creatures represent."

The Ashen hovered there, cloak streaming around him. Then he drifted toward the deck—toward me.

Normally, that'd be a bad thing.

My hand was still frozen in place by the pulsar staves. I pressed against the invisible gravity field holding me down. Straining. Demanding my fingers move. Because I leached whatever I could from my prosthetic leg, a storehouse of tachyon particles.

The staves ignited.

There was a tremendous boom, and a long whistle, followed by a huge splash not fifty feet from the edge of the ship. A geyser of water erupted.

"This is the United States Coast Guard!" The voice boomed through a megaphone. *"Heave to and prepare to be boarded!"*

Oh, great. So much for me waiting until the right moment.

I broke through the Ashen's gravitational grip and slammed into him like a human cannonball.

CHAPTER TWELVE

Score!

He didn't see that one coming.

It was just like I'd suspected—Word hadn't gotten too far out about the pulsar stave. Namely, that the weapon's energies could penetrate the gravitational warping of the medallions used by the Garrison and the Ashen. I'd seen Airfoil's fancy, ancient jewelry, and had a sneaky suspicion about its relation to the Hedron of Orbits, that sentient artifact that tried its best to wipe San Camillo off the map.

But I digress.

My attack on the Ashen guy—Warrior? Agent? Whatever.—sent us sprawling over the water-slicked deck. We spun around, grappling with each other, with him trying to reach for the pulsar staves and me straining to tap the medallion with the same weapon.

When I'd tried that on Airfoil, it had temporarily deactivated the medallion's powers.

Syndax mercs shouted at each other, I guess

unsure of where to aim, until gunfire drew their attention away. I saw Loredana drag Cordelia behind a bent section of the wreck's hull, as Randy shot at the mercenaries with both the TEC-9 and the Uzi. He stayed out in the open like an idiot, only kneeling when the return fire came his way, as sporadic and poorly aimed as it was.

The Ashen smashed his elbow across my jaw. Didn't see stars, but man, I wished I had, instead of feeling the pain. I broke from his hold and rolled sideways, as bullets splashed in the puddle we'd landed in. I flopped onto my back and fire a blast from the stave, sending the Syndax assailant pinwheeling across the deck.

"Moron!" The Ashen raised his hand.

"Nope!" I blasted at him with both staves.

He must have gotten a partial shield in place, because the energy beams went all distorted and wobbly before they flipped him over the torn deck.

Meanwhile, the cyber-spider skittered between the mercenaries, clawing at their legs, and even leaping atop one guy's masked face in a gut-churning imitation of everyone's favorite scary aliens. I took pity and blasted it clean off.

"Behind you!"

Loredana's warning brought me spinning around as a chunk of metal four feet across whipped toward my face like giant, razor edged Frisbee. I rejoined the stave and held it up, channeling as much power as I could through and into it.

The searing golden energies burned through the metal, shearing it in half, as molten bits hissed and burned against my wetsuit.

More gunfire—only this was a heavy, rhythmic shooting of a much larger gun. A long, slender Coast Guard cutter rode the waves, shooting at the fishing trawler. Which, it should be noted, not only attempted to shoot the cutter with machine guns but launched a couple rocket propelled grenades its way. Barely scratched the white hull.

The cannon on the bow of the cutter, though, *BOOMED.* The center of the trawler exploded in flame and fragments. Shadows jumped overboard.

"Surrender the wreck and prepare to be boarded!" Boy, the guy on the megaphone must really be having fun.

The Ashen snarled and hit me with what felt like a wall—like, one made of bricks. Since I've hit one face-first before, I knew the sensation, trust me. But then he twisted his right arm in a curling motion and punched the air.

Waves surged past the wreck. A big one out of the bunch changed course, by almost ninety degrees, and swept into the side of the cutter. It heeled over, water swamping its decks.

I struck back at the Ashen, opting for enhanced speed. In the space of a couple breaths, I sped across the deck, trying not to be distracted by the water droplets seemingly frozen midair. Hit the guy dead center in his chest. Had to sympathize with the muted *crack*, because my chest throbbed from where he'd knocked me a good one.

Two things.

First? The pulsar stave glanced off the guy's medallion. Lucky shot—or maybe the two relics were drawn to each other. Someday, I'd have to take a portal back to Meda and ask Teget. Figured my brother, busy safeguarding the temple of said relics, would know.

Anyway, metal *clinked* against metal, and the bubble trying to restrict me collapsed. The Ashen fell to his knees, gasping.

Second?

I abruptly remembered why he must be so exhausted, and how the wreck wasn't sinking.

Because he'd been using a gravitational field to keep it suspended above the waters.

The deck slanted. My feet slipped. So did a couple of Syndax guys, only they continued their slide until they bounced off the edge of the deck.

Loredana rushed from concealment, gloves outstretched, for the still immobilized cyber-spider. I say "immobilized" because it was in its hazy containment field, even if it was bouncing down the deck like a discarded basketball.

"The medallion!" I shouted.

Cordelia had me beat. She skidded on her knees beside the toppled Ashen, who was struggling to raise himself on wobbly elbow. Cordelia bashed him in the side of his head with her fists, and then tore at the front of his tunic. I could hear the fabric rip even through the rain, and over the groan of the submerging ship.

She yanked a silvery-gold emblem from a chain around his neck, hoisting it free.

Good deal. But we were still short one package. I scooped up the stasis initiator and fired it.

Bullseye. One more cyber-spider stuck in a cloud.

"I've got it." Loredana grappled with both frozen critters, her hair a tangle in front of her face. She grinned and brushed it aside with her elbow. "Now all we have to do is an admirable imitation of a dog paddle."

I gestured into the distance. The cutter had righted itself. Zodiacs dropped from its sides and raced toward the Syndax goons floating between the shipwreck and the destroyed fishing trawler, which had completely disappeared beneath the waves. "No kidding. Once we're aboard—"

A terrible rumble shuddered through the hull. The wreck lurched, throwing us aside. Loredana braced with her legs against the torn metal. I clung to her ankle. Cordelia, still hanging onto the Ashen and his medallion, banged shoulder-first into the same metal chunk.

Randy flew past us, limp as the proverbial noodle.

"No!" Cordelia almost dropped the medallion. "Catch him!"

He disappeared over the edge.

Wait. Was he unconscious? I thought I saw an

egg-sized lump on his forehead.

I knew what I had to do. I was the only one unencumbered. I glanced at Loredana.

"Go. I have this." She caught my lips in a fiery kiss. "I love you. And do not say, 'I know,' or you'll be stuck in stasis between our current samples."

I winked at her. "Love you, too."

Then I let go.

The water wasn't as cold a shock this time, because I slid in on purpose, but man, it sure hadn't gotten warmer. Mercury Hale, human popsicle.

Darkness closed in. Debris struck my shoulder.

Water.

I swirled around. Couldn't tell down from up, back from front.

A massive, shadowy bulk surged beneath—wait, so that was down. And there were ripples of white lights above, past the water's surface. Floodlamps?

Three rusted funnels yawned. Orange flames sparked from inside.

If it was under water, how was it on fire?

The bulk hurtled toward me, pushing the water aside in a torrent of bubbles.

Shipwrecks don't rise!

I swam for the surface, but even with the energies of the pulsar stave lingering in my body, I was too slow. Everything was too slow.

The arms shot up through the darkness, twisted amalgams of flesh and metal, stabbing through my chest.

Stop it!

I struggled to hold on to my breath. Grabbed for the pulsar staves. Their light broke through the surrounding gloom. Randy. I was down there to find Randy, before he drowned. No cyber-spider was around to attack. Loredana had them.

The shipwreck? Its bulk was overhead and a dozen yards away, settling deeper in the ocean. The orange lights were gone. It was a rusting skeleton. Nothing there could hurt me.

The pulsar staves illuminated metal. More debris? Nope. A gun. TEC-9.

Randy's boot drifted not far from it—a boot still containing a foot, linked to a slack body.

I plunged deeper, willing the pulsar stave's energies through my cells. There was nothing to fear. I knew how to swim. Knew where the surface was. My heart rate subsided into quick, steady beat. It got easier to hold my breath.

Well, not *that* much easier. I was still underwater.

I grabbed Randy around the chest. The hug was enough to jolt him awake. He thrashed in my grip, beating in my chest, until he blinked and saw who it was. Crazy fool grinned at me and gave a thumbs up.

Right. On.

I kicked for the surface, dragging Randy along. Lights glimmered. Searchlights from the cutter? Didn't matter. I could see smaller shapes flitting above, intercepting tiny silhouettes. People were getting picked up. One cluster looked like it had too many arms—Loredana, I hoped, and Cordelia.

What about the medallion? I'd channeled its might. Felt its power. Was it Procyon's now, since Cordelia took it off the Ashen guy?

Ancient forces beyond your ability to grasp, Mercury. Your time is ending.

Of all the—I ground my teeth. Fear swept through my body, my brain. Irrational terror. Everything that scared me, rolled into one. *Wasn't talking to you.*

It doesn't matter. We're a part of you. The Interstice links us. You draw on it; we inhabit it. It is us. And you're not the only one. Far from it. There are others who war in secret, or who dabble in the powers from beyond your dimension.

I gasped. Drank seawater. No. Not now. Not this close to the surface. The lights were just beyond reach. I mean, I only needed a few more inches—or was it dozens of feet?

I kept pushing. Reaching. My mind went haywire. I was gonna die—and with me, Randy. Two lives lost. To what? Fear? Why?

Deliver us from evil.

Please.

The pulsar stave's energy rippled up my legs, through my chest, out my arms. I shot up like cork, which, to be fair, I've never actually seen. Not a big wine drinker.

We broke the surface. The cutter's bow loomed in the distance, and the last of the funnels vanished beneath the waves.

"Mercury!" Loredana's red hair was a beacon from the cutter's stern—and so were the orange jackets of the Coasties with her. "He's over there!"

I whooped. Randy repeated his celebratory water slap, while spitting up water. "All right!"

"You're welcome." I spat out my own mouthful. "Next time, text an Uber."

"Yeah, you bet, but I bet they don't have the weapons of doom like us!"

I really didn't want to be bros, but I was glad we weren't dead.

Until we kept rising from the waters.

Not the Ashen. Not again.

But the invisible grip didn't mash us or tear us apart. Instead, it carried us as gently as if we were on Aladdin's carpet—and no, I didn't start singing "A Whole New World" because I wasn't sure if Randy would glare at me or join in.

We landed on the deck ahead of the pilothouse. Loredana hugged me the moment my feet touched down. "Thank heavens. When you didn't resurface—"

"It's okay. I made it. I'm good." I smiled at her.

"Really?" She brushed my hair, into goofy spikes, I was pretty sure.

"Yeah. Yeah, I am."

"He was great!" Randy slapped my back. This time, I didn't mind the sting. "Hey, Dee! We oughta hire this guy!"

"He's spoken for."

Aw, man. Hudson Bowe tipped his Homeland

baseball cap at me as he stepped forward with a couple of his generic agents and Cordelia. "You been busy, Mercury. I guess I owe you thanks for helping trounce Syndax—though as usual, we've got to clean up the mess."

I assumed he meant the dozen or so Syndax guys lined up in handcuffs along a bulkhead. The Ashen guy was there, too, mask in place. He trembled. "How about supervillains? You got a place to lock him up?"

Bowe shook his head and pointed up.

Another figure alighted on the roof of the pilothouse. Not a shrouded nightmare, but a ... guy. Light brown skin, crystal blue eyes, dark curly hair. He wore faded jeans and a nylon jacket, plus comfortable running sneakers, like he'd been out on a jog. He barely looked damp. "Good afternoon, all. Or evening, I suppose. It's an odd sensation, having jet lag without a jet."

"Who are you?" I tried to straighten up, like I was the man in charge, but my legs ached. I hoped he couldn't see me shaking.

"My name is Weld. Pleased to make your acquaintance. If you don't mind—"

He made a flicking motion with two fingers.

Cordelia gasped. The medallion hurtled from her belt pouch, into his waiting hand.

"I'll be taking that to its rightful owners."

"The Garrison," I said.

"No. It belongs to the Ashen. So they shall have

it. As for its owner, well, one can only surmise his fate given the magnitude of his failure, unless his superiors have a better use in mind." Weld snapped his other fingers. "That reminds me. You secured the creatures, I see."

I nodded. The cyber-spiders were shoved together in an immobile bundle on the deck. Loredana must have set them aside. I wondered what kind of container we could house them in until we got back to Hub the robotic suitcase for safe transport. "Might have to zap them into stasis again if it wears off."

"No bother." Weld curled his free fingers into a fist and twisted.

The cyber-spiders shriveled with a disgusting, crunching noise, their claws squelching in the water covering them. In a couple seconds, they were crushed into an unrecognizable, crusty mush. Then, those clumps just—went away.

"What have you done?" Loredana was on her feet, hands balled into fists. She'd probably have shot at the guy if she'd still had her gun.

Of course, that's what the Coasties looked like they were gonna do. Four aimed rifles skyward.

"Let's not, shall we?" Weld smiled. "My apologies, Mrs. Lark-Hale, but this incident has drawn our notice, and therefore, our intervention. The symmachites are too dangerous to be allowed continued existence, even for secure study in Procyon's hallowed halls. I'm sure your dead samples won't be an issue. It is the living which concern the Garrison."

"That wasn't part of the deal," Bowe muttered. "You showed up and told me—"

"I told you whatever was necessary to prevent you shooting at me." Weld flicked his fingers. The barrels of the Coasties' guns snapped off, clattering onto the deck. "A word of advice, Mercury Hale—Steer clear of these creatures and any of their ilk. I should hate to meet you as an enemy, given your assistance against the Ashen."

I sneered at him. "You meet me, you might wind up like him."

"Yes." Weld nodded. "We know."

The Ashen lifted from the deck, soaring limply over us until he was face to face with Weld. Then the pair swooped away into the clouds. I swore I heard a sonic boom. Or two.

"Blast," Loredana murmured.

"Hey." I patted her shoulder. "Could be worse. I really thought Weld would answer, 'I'm altering the deal. Pray I don't alter it any further.'"

Cordelia stared at me.

"*Empire Strikes Back.*" Randy, seemingly unbothered by the massive knot turning black and blue on his forehead, kept gnawing on a toothpick. Where did he get another one? And how was it still dry? "Nice one."

"Thanks."

We high-fived.

"I do believe," Loredana said, "That I am in need of a true vacation now."

CHAPTER THIRTEEN

Couldn't tell whether everyone was relieved or disappointed the cyber-spiders were destroyed. I mean, we could have found out a whole lot about the mutated species related to tiny, artificial microbes, the latter of which had brainwashed a bunch of my superhero friends right before our wedding.

Loredana, for her part, was placid as the sky outside the hotel conference room. Could be because she'd come to peace with our failure.

Or she could have been following my lead—keeping our mouth shut while Agent Bowe paced the room and railed at us.

"This is *exactly* why I tell my superiors that Homeland should sidestep Procyon!" he snapped. "Better yet, why you all should be locked up in Leavenworth or Gitmo or somewhere just as desolate."

"Nevada's pretty remote," I said. "I could

recommend a quiet town."

"You shut your trap!" Bowe shook his finger at me.

"Really? That's what you're gonna go with?" Remember how I said I was keeping my mouth shut? See how long that lasted? I waggled my finger back at him in exaggerated fashion. "This isn't high school and you're not our principal, Bowe. We stopped Syndax from stealing those creatures. Heck, we even disabled a member of the Ashen!"

Bowe winced.

"Oh, right, my bad." I rolled my eyes. "We're not supposed to talk about them. Like they're Voldemort. Look, I think we've all established that the Garrison and the Ashen exist, they're flying around out there, and they don't care one bit about our plans, because if they don't like them, they'll swoop in and tip the table over whenever they feel like it."

"That's another matter. It's above your pay grade, Mercury. So you keep yourself—"

"What was the arrangement you made?" Loredana's question was a soft, but firm, interruption.

"Beg your pardon?"

She gazed out the conference room window onto clear blue skies over a beach dotted here and there with umbrellas, pinpricks of color on white sand. Her hands, clasped behind her back, tapped a slow beat on her waist. "With the Garrison. Weld, as he called himself, countered the offer or arrangement or whatever you want to call it. What did you want from them, and vice versa?"

Bowe scowled.

Loredana looked over her shoulder, eyebrow raised.

"She's gonna keep asking," I mock whispered.

"You two are a colossal pain. Especially together." Bowe picked up a half-full glass of orange juice from our table and downed it like he was taking a shot of liquor. He wiped his mouth with the back of his hand. "Fine. All right. That Weld guy supposedly agreed to transfer the creatures—"

"Cyber-spiders." I raised my cup of coffee.

"To Homeland Security's custody. Had some way of taking them that wouldn't require your gun and your stave weapon." Bowe made a face like he'd stepped in dog turds while wearing his cowboy boots. "So much for that grand scheme."

I shook my head. "Hey, that's on you and the feds. We did our part. Like always. So, how about you quit treating us like terrorists and let us head home?"

Loredana joined me at the table, where she proceeded to butter a warm bagel. "I would hardly equate paying for a private breakfast with treating us like terrorists, Mercury."

"Well, maybe, but I bet the terrorists get yelled at less." I slugged coffee. Ah. Great warmth suffused my body. Even better than the pulsar stave's energies. Okay, close second.

"Doesn't matter now," Bowe said. "I was an

idiot."

"No argument there," I muttered.

He glared at me.

Loredana sighed. She poked me with a fork.

"What? He said it."

"Agent Bowe, I hope you'll forgive my operative, but our concern is understandably heightened now that the Garrison have shown themselves in a more public fashion than we're used to."

"This isn't the first time they've showed up and rubbed our faces in their powers," Bowe said. "I've got footage from Drake City … Never mind. Just know that Homeland's got them on their radar."

"I feel better already." I swirled the last of my coffee, trying for a miniature version of the whirlpool that the Ashen had used to toss a shipwreck up to the surface. "Look, I'm sure you guys have got your hands full with Syndax, when you're not chasing the more mundane terror threats. Why not let us lend a hand? You have to admit, we're pretty handy with those hands."

"Quite repetitive," Loredana said.

"Yeah, but I think he gets the idea."

Bowe snorted. "You guys and your gobs of money and your protection from—well, blazes, I don't even know who's got your back. All I know is, I got new orders to let you waltz out of this hotel like you'd just finished up your next honeymoon."

"Not a bad idea." I rounded the table and held out my hand. "Shake on it, partner."

He glared at my hand like he'd rather cut it off. "How's about you hunt your monsters, and I'll chase the humans."

"Sounds fair. Except if said humans are busy conjuring said monsters." I held up a finger and wagged it back and forth. "That's a big no-no in my book. They get the stave just like their astral fiend pets. Keep that in mind."

Bowe's phone buzzed at him. He glanced at the screen and rolled his eyes. Wow, he could give me a run for my money with that disgusted face. "Get out of here, you two. Best if we stay out of each other's ways."

Best idea I'd heard all week.

Cordelia was kind enough to give us a ride to the airport since, you know, we'd trashed our rental in the car chase and I didn't know about Loredana, but I had no desire to bounce along the expressway in the bed of Randy's truck, no matter how awesome a ride.

Loredana's jet sat on the tarmac outside a private hangar, perched for takeoff like it needed just the barest nudge from a pilot. She smiled. "Thank you for prepping her, Delia. Would I be surprised to find she's somewhat lighter of fuel in our absence this morning?"

"Sorry, Lori, I didn't have time for a joyride." Cordelia laughed. "It might not seem like it, but I do have bosses who expect reports. One, in particular.

Tyrone's not one to let a sixteen hundred miles dissuade him from a face to face talk."

"Video chat." Randy spat on the tarmac. "Makes me look fat."

"Could be the haircut," I said.

He chuckled and chewed on a toothpick.

"Have a safe flight." Cordelia embraced Loredana. Randy went in for a handshake, which Loredana returned just as firmly, while Cordelia pecked me on the cheek. "Good to see you again, Mercury. Take care of her."

"Doing my best." I winked at her.

She pressed a small, plastic object into my palm. "Light reading."

It was a flash drive, a third the size of a typical model—black and silver, no bigger than my thumbnail. I tucked it into my pants pocket, glancing at Loredana. She was smiling rather dryly at Randy's pontification on the best private aircraft engines. "This, ah, a group project?"

"Your eyes only."

"Very James Bond."

Cordelia's smile faded. "I'll leave it to you when to tell Loredana. There's a lot of background to Procyon that's been filtered out of the Historic Archives since 1848. I'm glad you came here. I'd thought about sending it to you but the time never seemed right."

She turned sidelong, shielding me, as Loredana approached. "Ready to go, Lori?"

"Indeed, though it has been a bracing visit."

Loredana raised an eyebrow. "Mercury?"

I saluted. "Co-pilot reporting, Mrs. Lark-Hale."

"Then let's not tarry. It's a long flight home."

She started for the airplane, Randy carrying our bags. I frowned at Cordelia. "Do I want to bother asking what's on the drive?"

"Sightings. Rumors. The scraps I've been able to gather about our pals the Garrison and the Ashen. I've spent too many years tiptoeing around their brawls—and then you show up, able to put one of them down. Break through his powers like they weren't there." Cordelia smirked. "Nothing I like better than new information."

"Yeah, but they know it, too."

"Which could give Procyon an advantage in the future. Guard it." Cordelia watched Loredana climb into the plane's cockpit. "And guard her."

I nodded, but really, I had no clue what she wanted me to do.

"Loaded up, Dee." Randy jogged back to us. His arm extended—

I spun past him and slapped him on the back.

Randy winced. He rolled his shoulder, but he grinned back, instead of, you know, shooting me. "Been waiting for that, haven't ya?"

"You know it." We shook hands. "Good luck out there, Randy."

"Thanks. Say, if I ever get bored chasing Syndax goons, I might roll to San Camillo and help you take out astral fiends."

"Sounds like fun. Make sure you bring a change of drawers for when they scare—"

"Okay, boys." Cordelia pulled on Randy's arm. "Come on. We've got a drug dealer's boat keys to return."

He chuckled. "Sure. With some flotsam out by Nassau, if he wants to go swimming for it."

They climbed into the Lincoln town car and drove off. Behind me, the Cirrus jet's engine rose into a whine.

"Kindly board!" Loredana shouted. "Unless you're planning to walk to California!"

"No way!" I jogged over, shoes splashing through a puddle, grateful to be alive and glad to put a lot of things behind me—like the terror the depths, and the factions warring over ancient medallions.

But not the mystery.

A couple hours into our flight west, after we'd exhausted idle chit-chat, Loredana cleared her throat.

Uh-oh.

"If I may ask," she said. "What did Cordelia give you."

"It wasn't a good-bye kiss," I blurted.

Loredana raised an eyebrow.

"Kidding. I mean, that's true." I scratched the back of my neck. "You saw?"

"She and I underwent similar training in our early Procyon days. While my grasp of espionage is not as thorough as hers, I can recognize a subtle passing of an object."

I blew out a breath. Operationally, the contents of the flash drive were mine to keep secret. But it was Loredana. My handler. More importantly, my wife. "It's information. I haven't looked at it yet. She told me—"

Loredana shook her head. "I trust you to tell me when you're ready. But if Cordelia meant it for you, then you must ascertain whether it is information you should share or not. I won't demand it. I know her too well."

"Thanks. That'll make it easier."

She smiled. "How are you feeling?"

I chuckled. "Same as the other four times you asked. Seriously, though—good. Better than good. It's like, I needed that to get rid of the fear. Sure, the dregs are still hanging around, but I had to face it before I could rip it to shreds."

Of course, I didn't feel like I'd done it alone. Ramos had helped. He always did.

Him, and his faith.

Weird. I shifted in my seat. Metal clinked against the flash drive. "Hey, I almost forgot." I dug into my pocket. "Picked this up at the hotel gift shop this morning."

I pressed the triangle into her palm. She laughed at the miniature pizza, yellow and brown with three red circles. "It's adorable. But am I to trade it as a chit if I want to share a pie with you?"

"Turn it over."

A simple phrase was engraved on the backside: "I love you more than pizza."

"High praise." She kissed me. "I love you, too."

I grabbed a tablet from one of our bags behind my seat and fired it up. No time like the present. "More than *Dr. Who?*"

"Well …"

I chuckled as I inserted the drive into the USB port. A folder opened. It was filled with dozens and dozens of more folders, each one stuffed with files. They were labelled with jumbled letters and numbers. I tapped on one. My eyes widened. "I … wow."

"What is it?" Loredana grimaced. "No, wait—I said you didn't have to share."

Cordelia's advice went right out the window as surely as if I'd cracked the canopy. "Oh, I think I'd better." I twisted the tablet.

The image I'd opened was a scan of a black and white photograph. The subject? A chunk of tree bark, big as a waiter's serving tray, judging by the spectacled young man with the slicked back hair holding. A cyber-spider, or a rough approximation of it, was carved in rough strokes, by either a metal or stone implement.

Except the cyber-spider towered over a bunch of slender warriors with spears and bows wearing next to nothing, but lots of paint—side by side with Spanish conquistadors.

The scribbled notation at the corner of the

photograph said *1903*.

"I suggest you keep your findings to yourself, until you've had the chance to research them thoroughly,"she said.

"Yeah." I gazed at the young guy who looked just as perturbed by the carvings as I felt. "Because finding out the symmachites had bigger and badder brothers could be the least of our problems."

Mercury's adventures continue...

Stay tuned

www.steverzasa.com

Winner of the 2020 Realm Makers Award: Middle Grade

Whether they're saving their neighborhood from rampaging plastic toys brought to life, or keeping superpower-inducing fizzy drinksaway from bullies, brothers Iggy and Oz Risner need all the help they can get!

Author J.J. Johnson

https://amzn.to/3mlq5Cu